two kinds
of silence

two kinds
of silence

mark blayney

manuscript

First published 2003
by Manuscript Publishing
41 Southview Road
Marlow
Bucks
SL7 3JR

British Library Cataloguing in Publication Data
A CIP record for this book is available from the British Library.

ISBN 0 9545505 1 X

Printed and bound by The Cromwell Press, Trowbridge, Wiltshire.
Cover design by Anna Mullin.

For Pip

contents

two kinds of silence

I

He was dubious about the boat trip because he couldn't swim, but as it was his honeymoon he agreed. Emily went in to book it as she was better at that kind of thing, whilst Manfred watched a stray dog nose around the stone walls, desiring interesting smells rather than unlikely scraps of food. At a distance, two enormous old women dressed in black stood motionless in a doorway, watching Manfred. He met their gaze and smiled half-heartedly. One of them absently adjusted her veil.

The beads rustled behind them as a child, naked but for a pair of pants, ran out and chased the dog down the road. The boy kicked up balls of dust and the women looked idly after him, making no effort to move, until they both slowly disappeared behind the dust as if they were ghosts.

Manfred jumped as he felt a hand on his shoulder. 'He wants to talk to you,' Emily said. She looked round at the sun-blenched street, blinking in the light.

'What?'

Emily looked back at him earnestly. 'The man in the shop, he wants to speak to you.'

'Oh, okay,' said Manfred uncertainly. He followed her through the doorway and his eyes took a few seconds to adjust to the gloom. He put his hands out, somehow imagining that he was about to overbalance. When the room came into view he saw Emily looking at him with concern. Even when his eyes had got used to the light, the room seemed gloomy and too dark for comfort; Manfred had to look at everything carefully in order to see it. There was a large heavy wooden table, flaking dark green walls and a bulge in the ceiling where some stuffing was emerging like a burst mattress.

Behind the table was Kem, a short, athletic man in grey shirt, black jeans and square black sunglasses. In shorts and T-shirt, Manfred was collecting pools of water in his armpits, groin and along the length of his back; Kem's skin shone but did not sweat, despite the heavy clothes.

Behind Kem, an enormous map of the stretch of coastline where they were staying appeared from the gloom. Manfred had thought it was a large dirty canvas, but now he could trace the outlines of land and sea, appearing on his retina like a photograph developing. The map had faded Polaroids of turtles and ruins stuck to it and was such large scale that had he not known where he was, Manfred would not recognise what country it was supposed to be.

Emily sat down and Manfred saw there was another chair for him. He sat in it and put his hands on his knees and kept his mouth shut. In front of him were two steaming glasses of tea. The glasses looked like vases for tiny flowers, and the tea like a fine tawny port. Manfred felt his mouth water, but watched the glass intently, as if suspicious it might move. He did not want to be under any obligation to go anywhere just because he had been given tea. But Emily picked her glass up and enthusiastically drank it, nodding encouragingly to Kem. Begrudgingly, Manfred picked his flower vase up and sipped at it. He grimaced and set it back on the table.

'Where would you like to go?' With a sweep of his hand Kem

indicated the map behind him; it might have been the whole world. Manfred nodded politely and put the virtually untouched tea down. Kem noticed. 'You don't like it?' he said concernedly, pointing at it.

'Yes, it's very nice, thank you.'

'I tell you what.' Kem reached forward and picked up the two small cubes of sugar that Manfred had not noticed by the side of the glass.

'No I don't have sugar in tea – '

Kem dropped the sugar into the glass. 'Try now,' he said. 'Try it, try it!'

Manfred tried it. He glanced at Kem who was watching him with anticipation. 'That's really good,' Manfred said, thoroughly surprised. Kem sat down heavily in his chair and thumped the cane arms with satisfaction. 'I tell you so!' he exclaimed. 'You like more?'

'Yes please,' said Emily in a quiet voice, pushing her empty glass forward. Manfred looked at her in surprise; she would normally have shaken her head demurely at such a question. Emily, unaware of his look, pointed to the map. 'Can we go here?' she said timorously, pointing to the picture of a turtle, which was stuck over a long inlet of water.

'Of course you can my friends,' Kem said expansively.

'It looks a very long way,' said Manfred doubtfully.

'No, no, no, this is very large map, is not as far as it looks. A very reasonable price for the day's trip, too.'

Emily tried to read the garbled caption under the picture. It was in English, but it didn't make much sense. 'Does it say this is a turtle beach?' she asked.

'Yes,' Kem said, his eyes narrowing knowledgeably. 'The turtles travel long distances to lay their eggs on this particular stretch of beach. No one knows why, they are very fussy about it, it has to be this particular beach. At certain times of year the beach is cordoned off to protect the turtles.'

'Oh, it's not cordoned off at the moment, is it?'

'No, no, of course not.' Kem opened his eyes wide.

'I would love to see turtles,' she said quietly. Kem rifled about in his desk and found a long cane. Drawing it out, he pointed it like a weatherman and rapped it importantly on the map. 'This is the turtle beach, and here you see very important tombs of bygone ages, carved into the rock face.'

'Oh, good,' said Manfred.

'It will take about hour to reach the tombs, then you have hour visit, then hour or so to come back, everything is included in the price, you have good lunch and good time, and then you come back, and this trip is tomorrow, okay?'

'Tomorrow?' said Manfred, standing up and panicking as if he would have to rush home and pack at once.

'Well,' said Emily, standing up too, 'that sounds very exciting.'

A gold tooth flashed as Kem smiled back.

'That one looks a bit noisy,' she said, 'I don't want to go there.'

'How about this one?'

'That's a bit empty.'

As they hovered, a waiter quickly emerged from inside. 'You like to come in, beautiful lady?' he said.

'We're just looking, thanks,' replied Emily.

They walked on. 'You have a little think, and you come back,' called the waiter. 'I make you wonderful meal.'

They were near the end of the street. After another three or four shops the buildings became squatter and more run down. Beyond that, the road disintegrated into broken walls and scrub and the gravel broke up into a dirt track. On the corner was the phone box with its yellow sign hanging limply and drunkenly on one screw, and beyond that a small triangle of sea.

A truck hurtled down the hill ahead and passed them, two fountains of dust spiralling into the air behind it. The inhabitants of the back of the truck laughed and screamed as they bounced up and down on the road and clutched the sides for dear life. The enormous wheels rumbled past Emily and Manfred and they shaded their eyes and coughed.

There was one more restaurant before the village ceased to exist, but Emily still balked.

'It looks okay,' he said encouragingly.

'Yes, all right then.' She changed her mind as they walked up to the door; no waiter came out to greet them, so she decided it must be indifferent and probably have slow service.

'Why don't we go back to that last one?' Manfred suggested. 'At least he was friendly.'

She twisted her lip. 'They're all friendly. That's how they get you to go inside.'

'Well, I know,' he said. He ignored the slowly growing gnawing exasperation. She didn't like the ones where someone tried to coax them in because they were pushy, but she didn't like the ones where no one tried to coax you in because they were indifferent. If they were empty she didn't want to go in because there must be something wrong with them, but if they were full she didn't want to go in because they were too busy.

'Where do you want to go then?' It came out too sharply. He had an image of Emily having an image of him putting his hands on his hips and challenging her to come up with a better idea. It was not supposed to sound like that and he looked obliquely at her in anticipation of her getting cross. They had not yet had an argument. The honeymoon seemed the likeliest place for it to happen.

'Well,' she said, looking round a little forlornly, 'yes, let's go back to that last one.' She looked back towards it. The dust from the truck hung in a haze in front of it, moving slowly. 'Even though it is empty.'

'At least we'll get good service,' he reasoned, taking her arm quickly before she could change her mind. The waiter welcomed them like prodigal children. 'I knew you would come back, my friends,' he said, showing them to the best table, in the centre of the courtyard under an overhanging olive tree. 'Beautiful lady sit here,' he said, 'and I get you menus.' He ran happily to the kitchen.

Emily was still cautious, worried they had made the wrong choice. 'Do you think the food will be all right?' she whispered.

'Of course it will,' he whispered back.

The waiter busied himself putting napkins on their laps and fussing around Emily, asking her if the candle was too bright, or if she would like more candles; checking her seat was near enough to the table, or maybe it was too far away; asking if she was warm enough, or perhaps it was too hot? Emily, pretending not to enjoy this attention, told him everything was fine and frowned a little, but smiled enough to ensure he would come back before too long.

'I'm glad we came here,' said Emily decisively. Manfred nodded slowly. In the future would he find Emily fussy and irritating? He agreed readily to everything at the moment, but would he have the patience in a year's time to wander up and down streets rejecting restaurants until they found one that she was happy with?

They're all the same anyway, he thought as her watched her look round contentedly. They all serve steak, defined as a greyish, soft cut of meat that had a tart, fragrant flavour and tasted good but bore no relation to what would be called steak at home; and scampi. The more adventurous restaurants served sea bass, tuna and if you were lucky, squid. They also all sold Albanian liver, a delicacy they had so far managed to avoid. But Manfred knew that you could go into any one of them and be sure of an excellent meal, exceptionally friendly service, and a reasonable price.

This was what you would think at home, anyway. If any of these restaurants were in an English town, they would be the best in the district. Emily, however, was one of those people who have to consider everything that is on offer before making a final decision based on careful consideration of all the options. The fact that any of the options were better than what you could expect elsewhere was neither here nor there.

The waiter brought the wine. Emily was still looking around vacantly. The waiter tipped the first mouthful or so into a small bowl and put the bowl on an adjoining table. 'You know what you like?' he said.

'Oh, gosh, we haven't even looked,' said Emily apologetically, quickly picking up the menu.

'No,' said the waiter, raising his hands and shaking them as if buffing headlamps, 'you take as long as you like. I bring you some salad, or fish, while you think.' Emily nodded. She smiled at Manfred, who couldn't help smiling back; maybe she was right after all. He looked at the branches, lazily overhanging the pots which dangled on rusting hooks in the crumbling wall. He studied the gourds and water vessels lined up beneath, and the rough mosaic of glazed blue and green tiles that decorated the low wall behind Emily, and the baked brick floor.

The waiter came back with mussels, octopus and calamari, crab paste and a salad rich in tomatoes, olive oil and hoummus. Emily clapped her hands and looked at it in wonder like a child at Christmas. The waiter, charmed by this display, bowed in pleasure and liberally topped up Emily's wine glass.

'Oh don't,' said Emily, 'I'll get tipsy.'

'You are on holiday,' said the waiter, 'you are allowed to.'

'Yes,' agreed Manfred, 'we're on our honeymoon, actually.' He helped himself to wine.

The waiter put his hands together and sighed. 'Your honeymoon. How wonderful.' He touched Emily briefly on the shoulder before leaving. Emily giggled. 'Your face!' she said to Manfred.

'What?' said Manfred, trying to keep his face blank.

13

She giggled again.

The waiter took their orders. Emily deliberated over the starters while Manfred asked for meze and bass; after the waiter coaxed and persuaded and recommended and laughed and cajoled, Emily plumped for king prawns and steak.

'Can't be doing with all this funny sounding foreign stuff,' she said after he had gone. 'You need to know where you stand with food on holiday; you don't want to end up being ill.' Manfred nodded.

A family of four appeared and the waiter bolted through the whitewashed doorway and past Emily and Manfred to greet them. By the archway, the older child picked at the crumbling brick, looking with wonder at how easily it came away from the wall. She examined her fingernails and rubbed the grit between her fingers. The father tugged her away from the wall and into the restaurant. 'Hello, wonderful family,' said the waiter, and Manfred and Emily smirked.

'Come in, come in, I have a beautiful table for you over here.' He settled them as he talked. 'You want drinks, you like birra, you like wine? I have orange juice for the children. What is your name?'

'Elizabeth,' the girl said nervously.

'Elees...'

'Elizabeth.'

'Elees, aabuth.' The waiter opened his mouth wide as he emulated her; his eyes bulged and when he went he turned and winked at her. Elizabeth laughed and looked up at her mother for approval. The waiter went through the whitewashed doorway, loudly muttering 'Leesabuth, Leesabuth.'

Manfred ate his meze thoughtfully and quietly, enjoying the different flavours. Emily wondered what he was thinking; he looked preoccupied. She listened to his careful chewing and occasionally stuck her fork into his food to taste it. He smiled when she did this, so she did it more frequently.

'Hello,' she said softly. Manfred glanced up at her and then down to where she was looking. A child aged about three stood by the side of the table, his fair curly hair just visible from where Manfred was sitting. He leant across. The child looked up with large, pale blue eyes. 'Hello,' he said in a tiny voice, tugging at the table legs. He smelt of fresh washing powder. His face and hair were so pale that Emily felt an instinct to put a sun hat on him, even though it was cool and shaded in the restaurant.

'What's your name?' Emily asked.

'Momo,' said the child. 'Momo.'

'Michael,' said the mother, firmly if not sharply. 'Michael, come back.' The child trotted obediently to his mother. Emily smiled at her, to show they hadn't been disturbed. The mother busily attached the child to his chair with a series of straps. Michael struggled unhappily, then gave up without any noise and accepted imprisonment.

'He's lovely isn't he,' Emily said wistfully.

'Mmm.' Manfred finished his meze, chasing some juice and small leaves around the dish and dipping bread into the remains. Emily looked at him carefully. 'A child like that would be wonderful,' she said.

'Yes,' he murmured, 'but you never know what you're going to get, do you? You might get something completely awful.'

She nodded. The waiter came back and took their plates away. 'Is good?' he said, his eyebrows low in his forehead. 'You enjoy?' Emily nodded vigorously at him, her lips tightly closed.

Manfred was too preoccupied with the boat trip to think about children. He was beginning to regret what he committed himself to, but there was no getting out of it now. Nor did he feel able to talk to Emily about it. Emily filled her wine glass and watched the children. Every time the waiter came back the girl shouted 'Elizabeth, Elizabeth' at him, and he pretended still not to be able to say it. 'Ellybuth,' he said. 'Elzybeth.' She banged her fists on the wooden table in delight.

Emily looked at Manfred, who was cupping his wine glass with his hands and rotating it, watching the fluid move about inside. Had she made a terrible mistake, she wondered. 'They're so friendly, aren't they,' she said loudly. Manfred looked up. 'I mean,' she continued, 'these people invade their pretty town and they're so welcoming.'

She drained her glass and filled it up again; a little splashed over the side. 'I stayed in this bed and breakfast in Brighton once and the woman was so rude, you wouldn't think she wanted anyone to stay with her at all.'

Manfred tried to think of an answer to this. He rehearsed a few things in his mind but they all sounded trivial and banal, so he said nothing. Emily's brow furrowed. 'Are you all right?' she murmured.

He looked up, as if caught out over something. He nodded, and put his hand over hers.

Manfred opened his wallet and took out some multicoloured notes. 'They're very exotic, aren't they?' commented Emily, taking a red one and looking at the unknown hero on the front. 'Much more interesting than our boring old ones.'

Manfred examined the purple, red and brown notes, trying to work out which was the one he needed. The waiter hovered over him.

'It's difficult when everything's in so many millions,' he murmured, 'to work out which one you want.' Manfred pulled out several of the red ones, which he had established were worth about five pounds each.

The waiter leant in closer to him. 'You have English pounds,' he said, his eyes large and wide as he looked at the hologram of the £20 note glinting up at him. 'I take English pounds.' His hand stayed near the wallet, ignoring the offered notes.

'It's okay,' said Manfred, waving the red bills at him. 'I've worked it out now.'

'The first time I tried to pay for anything,' Emily was saying, 'I thought I'd given the man fifty thousand and I'd actually given him five hundred thousand. And he got upset and gave it back to me, and I thought how nice of him – ' her nose wrinkled – 'because he could easily have kept it and I'd never have known.'

'Right.'

'And then I realised I should have given him five million.'

'Mmm,' Manfred nodded.

The waiter took the three red notes. 'Thank you,' he said in his careful, waxy voice. He bowed to Emily. 'And thank you beautiful lady.' He winked at her and walked away.

Manfred fell asleep immediately. Emily lay awake, listening to the air conditioning gently purring. They were both naked under the thin sheet. Emily was still unsure about sleeping naked but it did not seem to bother Manfred, so she went along with it; she was on holiday. After lying awake for an hour she lifted the sheet and padded across the marble floor. The distances seemed a lot further in the dark, she thought as she reached the unguarded steps. Must never walk out here when tipsy, she told herself, running her hand along the stone wall to assure herself she was not about to plunge off the edge.

She walked across the warm tiles to the kitchen and found the fridge by touch; opening it, she removed the bottle of water. By the light of the fridge she opened the cupboard and took out a glass. She drank a glassful in one draught then filled it up again, replaced the bottle and felt her way back up the stairs.

Emily dreamt of turtles. She swam towards one and touched its bony shell and its wizened head, which felt like a walnut. The turtle opened its mouth and told her it loved her. In the morning she would remember the dream and feel embarrassed. She often dreamt about animals talking; this was the kind of thing Manfred would find silly, and she knew she could never talk to him about it.

She slept with her legs entwined in his and her arm across his chest. About six o'clock, when the land started to heat up but before the sun rose, she woke and could not get back to sleep. She pushed back the thin white sheet and stared up at the ceiling fan, and listened to its slow, rhythmical whoosh as it moved round like an old aeroplane propeller when it is being pushed but not accelerating. She turned onto her side and rested her hand gently on Manfred's naked arm, not wanting to wake him. She rubbed the hairs delicately, watching them stand up and then fold neatly down again when she pushed them the wrong way.

Through the square of window behind him, Emily saw the sky above the sun lose its hollow greyness and begin to swell with the rich yellows and purples of sunrise, like an orchestra developing melodies before the main theme. As she watched, a red point of light appeared above the blueish fuzz of trees on the horizon. The sky continued its fast-moving build-up, clouds sweeping across the rapidly shifting tones of mauve and red. There was even a band of green, flashing across the sky like an illusion, before the red circle of the sun heaved above the trees and lobbed into the sky.

Emily watched Manfred breathing shallowly. The glistening ball of the sun hovered behind him as if balancing on his chest. Emily thought he looked beautiful. The tiny hairs on his stomach and around his jaw were golden, picked out individually as if under a microscope. Perhaps today would be a better day, she thought. She got out of bed and walked silently downstairs.

She pulled the white muslin drape to one side and was surprised to see the sun free of the horizon and several degrees up in the sky. It had lost its fierce redness and was now a burnished, mellow orange; it seemed a miracle that all this could happen in a few seconds. It reminded her of orange cream chocolates and her mouth watered.

The sun developed swimming shapes on its surface as she stared at it; she turned away and blinked at the fridge, which had a large purple sun imprinted on it.

Manfred stood in the doorway and watched her. She pushed the door of the fridge shut and his eye followed her hand back to the tomatoes and lettuce she was dicing on the table. He watched the muscles in her arm pulsing as she chopped the vegetables with careful, equal pauses between each rhythmical slice. It was as if there were a musical pattern to her movements; after a while she started humming to herself. His eye travelled down the ridge of her spine and he smiled as she gently swayed, dancing in time to the tune she was humming, her buttocks moving alternately up and down and her pink painted toes tapping on the stone floor.

She tossed the salad in a large bowl and drizzled some olive oil over it. She sliced some bread and ran honey over it then added a small pool of honey on the side of the plate. Finally she sliced another two oranges and put them on a smaller plate. She put the honey and the rest of the bread back in the fridge, wiggling her bottom as she murmured the rest of the song and closing the door with a languorously stretched foot.

Turning, she saw Manfred. She did not jump or say 'you frightened me,' or 'what on earth are you doing creeping around like that,' as other people might have done. 'I've made some breakfast,' she said quietly.

II

They sat naked on the balcony, nervously wondering if anyone might come out of the other villas and see them, but too lazy to go back upstairs and put clothes on. They were both silent as they ate their meal. He took the heavy china plates out to the kitchen and rinsed them, listening to the pleasant sounds of running water against the thick ceramic and the ceramic against the stone sink.

'I'm really looking forward to the trip,' she said, taking her sarong from the back of the chair and tying it round her waist. He nodded. 'Me too.' He laid the plates with a clatter at the side of the sink. He felt nervous, but told himself not to worry about the boat. You have to live, you're on your honeymoon, you have to do things you don't normally do, he told himself.

They walked through the street which was deserted apart from a naked child making patterns in the dust. In the bay, wooden gulets and pleasure boats bobbed up and down, tied to the shore by thick gnarled ropes. In the silence of early morning Manfred and Emily could hear the creaking of the boats gently moving in the water, the pine expanding and contracting, like a plank stretching in hot sunlight. They walked along the quay, trying to work out which boat was the right one. They all looked the same; a flotilla of ships, the red flag with the little white crescent fluttering proudly from each mast.

They held hands as they waited for someone to point them to the right boat. 'We're a bit early,' Emily reassured Manfred as he looked anxiously around. He clenched and unclenched the hand that was not clinging onto Emily. He felt a surge of uncertainty in the pit of his stomach as they walked along the rickety ladder suspended from the quay to the boat.

Once aboard, this feeling disappeared and they wandered

about, enjoying the sensation of their feet on the sprung wooden floor. The top deck was already full of Germans, who occupied all the sun loungers and were well on their way to deep and painful scarlet tans. Emily and Manfred sat in the belly of the boat which was virtually empty, the only occupant being a lithe sleek youth of about nineteen who sat on a wooden chest under sponges which dangled immediately above his head.

As the boat slowly chugged its way from the dockside the sponges juddered and swayed and knocked into the boy's head, but he did not seem to mind. The boat swung round 180 degrees to head out into the harbour and a diagonal line of bright sunlight swept across the centre of the boat until it illuminated the boy's burnished, beautiful face. He read a newspaper leisurely, slowly turning each page after he had read everything on it.

Emily sat opposite Manfred on the seat, which reminded her of a pub bench; wooden planks bolted either side of a tabletop pitted with knotholes. She squeezed his hand as the boat moved quickly into the centre of the bay, then its speed dropped as it left the green fuzz of headland behind and plotted a course parallel to the coastline.

Someone swung down the wooden ladder, which creaked under his pressure. Manfred looked up and was surprised to see it was Kem. Manfred had a bizarre image of Kem being here and in the shop at the same time. Perhaps they were twins. 'Hello my friends,' said Kem.

'Do you think we'll see turtles?' Emily asked in a quietly excited voice. Manfred tried unsuccessfully to see Kem's eyes under his sunglasses. 'If we are lucky we will; maybe if we are not lucky, we won't.' He spoke in a sing-song voice with an enigmatic smile behind the impenetrable glasses.

After half an hour Emily went to sit at the front of the boat. Manfred could just see her along the side of the passageway, past the toilet, talking to the boy with the sponges, who was fiddling with ropes. He didn't seem to grasp what Emily was saying, but raised no objection when she took her sarong off, draped it on the floor in a tight corner of the boat and lay down. He jumped over her from time to time when he needed to get back in the boat. Kem would click his fingers from time to time and the boy would look up in a daze then scurry off to the bow or up the rickety wooden staircase to do whatever Kem told him to do. Every few minutes he would be back again, carefully reading his paper.

Manfred got up and went to talk to Emily.

The boat chugged slowly across the bay. There was a distant white growth on the shore to their left; a large town. Emily unfolded the map from her guidebook and studied it to see what the town was called. Looking over her shoulder with her hair blowing up to his face in the breeze, Manfred failed to see how it could apparently take such a short amount of time to get to the turtle beach; surely it could not be as little as an hour. It seemed a very long way indeed.

At the start of the honeymoon, Manfred had worked distances out on the map the way he did at home; he had thought they would be able to visit plenty of places. But this did not take into account how mountainous the landscape was and how bad the roads were. It could take an hour and a half just to travel twenty or thirty miles, if there was a steep mountain road to wind to the top of and then get all the way down again. So he could not see how a trip in a small, slow boat could cover the kind of distance that had taken all day by road.

But perhaps he was wrong; Kem should know what he was talking about, and Manfred accepted that he was not very good at judging distances. Perhaps boats were faster.

Feeling the sun on his neck, Manfred went back inside. Two men in their late twenties with hairy faces and large bellies sat at one of the tables. Beside them were two silent, beautiful girls. The men spread tabloid newspapers out in front of them. Manfred, feeling a sudden pleasurable sensation of how amazing it was to be here and how different everything was, sat opposite them on one of the little wooden seats and nodded. The men nodded back and concentrated on the papers.

'Er – do you speak any English?' Manfred asked. The first one, who was completely bald on his head but compensated for this by being covered in thick luxurious hair on his shoulders, shrugged. The second man scratched his head. 'A little,' he said, tipping his hand from side to side. Manfred nodded, unable to think of anything else to say.

The two men picked their ears, yawned and looked out of the window. The endless monotonous surf passed by. The boat had been travelling for nearly an hour. Flying fish shot across the water, leaping up from beneath the boat as if by magic. The sun reflected on their backs and made them look like pebbles being skimmed.

Manfred watched the girls, who looked tired and bored. One was blonde and bronzed with a concave stomach and breasts that defied gravity. The other, less tall, less curvaceous and more bored, sniffed.

'Are you here to see the turtles?' he asked her.

The man next to her shrugged. 'We are on holiday, you know,' he said.

'Where do you live?' He aimed his question at both of them. 'Istanbul,' the man said.

The girls rested their heads on their hands and stared out of the window, not understanding the English conversation or not interested. Manfred suspected the latter.

He kept the conversation going. 'I haven't been to Istanbul,' he announced.

'Is very nice. Is very hot. Is very full of people. Is good. You go.'

Manfred looked at the hairy man, who flipped the paper over to read the sports pages. Manfred turned round and saw Emily, basking in the sunlight of the front of the boat, holding court in front of a group of men who eagerly crowded round her. She lay on a towel and chatted away quite happily, shading her eyes from the sun, apparently oblivious to the fact that they did not seem to understand much of what she was saying. For their part, they nodded and smiled, not worrying too much how much they took in but keen for her to carry on talking. A cloud appeared in the sky. It was noticeable in the vast, empty blue sky because it was the first one Manfred had seen since the honeymoon had begun. Thin and fast-moving, its component wisps drifted apart. Eventually it vanished.

One of the girls moved up the bench to the bald hairy man, rested her head in his neck and closed her eyes. She nuzzled against him and murmured things to him from time to time but he made no effort to talk back and concentrated on the paper, his mouth occasionally mouthing the words he read. After a while both girls fell fitfully asleep, listening to the hypnotic chug of the engine. Their boyfriends made their way systematically through the newspapers. Eventually Kem opened up a locker in the centre of the boat, which turned out to be a fridge, and the men bought four bottles of beer.

The boat headed towards an attractive, quiet bay. The water was a dark oily green, marbled with white streaks like veins in jade. The boat slowed and Manfred thought this meant they were nearly there.

'Okay,' announced Kem, 'and now we all stop for the swimming break.'

From above, there was the thunder of Germans leaping up and stampeding down the stairs. Manfred watched as they took bags out of previously invisible wooden hatches and found swimming hats, goggles, sun cream. The narrow corridor alongside the toilet became blocked with three enormous women, who squeezed up against each other, queuing for the narrow exit. Areas of fat attempted to squeeze into the spaces left by other rolls of fat travelling in the opposite direction, like amoebae splitting off and then coming into contact with other amoebae.

The engine stopped. The sponge boy dropped the anchor and the Germans scrambled up to the entrance. Kem lowered the boarding ramp and the women used this as their diving board. Each time one of them leapt off, the boat bobbed up and down in the water like a cork.

Emily, to the untrained observer a fully dressed woman, removed her top and sarong and was immediately transformed into a girl in a bikini. Manfred scratched his head and looked down at his shorts and trainers.

Emily grinned. 'Not joining me in a swim?'

He shook his head.

'Why not?'

He folded his arms, unable to tell her. She shrugged and jumped into the water; the boat did not rock and sway when she leapt off in the way it had done with the others.

'Come on,' she called to him, treading water. Her body was white and perfect against the shifting green water.

'I can't,' he said, his voice wavering as he tried to think of a reason. 'Er – I haven't brought any swimming stuff.'

'Why not?' she called back, smiling.

'I didn't think it was that kind of trip.'

'Just do it in your pants!' She splashed about and laughed as a young man swam underneath her legs and emerged immediately in front of her, spraying water. She swam away from him and bobbed about a little distance away, looking up at Manfred, her expression losing its hopefulness. Manfred watched the water foaming and heaving around her.

He sat inside the empty boat, enjoyed the isolation and flicked through Emily's guidebook. At least, he reflected, exploring the turtle beach would be an experience worth endurance; with this in mind he resolved to be as patient as necessary. It was to be expected that it would take several hours to get there and not what they had been told. He did not really mind.

The cacophony of Germans leapt and yelped and screamed and giggled their way around the boat until they surrounded it like a school of whales. Emily swam sleekly between them, a slender fish sparkling in the water and darting about quickly in case she got eaten or squashed.

Manfred watched her. Laughing and joking, she chatted away excitedly to the two girls who had been completely silent when he had tried to speak to them.

Emily swam back towards the entrance to the boat. Manfred watched the sun glistening on her blue nylon skin. She looked like a dolphin emerging from the water. He worried about whether they had enough in common. She looked beautiful and immortal as she swam through the water and the sun glittered on the smooth blue lines of her bikini. But in ten years' time, he wondered uncertainly, will we have anything to say to each other? Already there were long silences between them. He supposed that all newly-married couples have their doubts. He wondered what she thought.

He smelt something burning and glanced up. At the front of the boat, the sponge boy was standing in front of a giant skillet, which was strapped to the prow like an Iron Age figurehead. A flame from a gas canister under the skillet played around its blackened, crusted base and clouds of black smoke billowed from the top as the boy poured olive oil into it. He started throwing in large pieces of chicken.

Emily jumped onto the suspended steps and came through the hatch at the front of the boat. She padded over to Manfred, leaving perfect wet footprints on the dusty dry pine floor of the boat.

'Hello,' he said. She shook her hair out, showering him with a fine spray of water. 'It's marvellous out there,' she said, 'lovely and warm.'

He nodded. She looked like a different person when she had been swimming; she was bolder and spoke more confidently.

'Smells like the food is almost ready.' She stood in front of him, drying herself and breathing rapidly. 'Oh, I feel so much better for that.'

He nodded.

'I'm going to stand out in the sun to dry off,' she said. 'But tell me if they serve lunch, okay?'

She ruffled her hand through his hair and his scalp tingled with the cold wetness from her hand. She padded back to the front of the boat where a knot of men parted admiringly to let her pass.

The boy chopped some vegetables up roughly, added these to the skillet and stirred the mixture absently while staring out to sea. He boiled some water in a large oval bucket, swinging a kind of grille out below the skillet and balancing the bucket on it so that it was above the flame. He tipped pasta into the water from a paper parcel.

Meanwhile the tables inside the boat filled up rapidly and Manfred found himself separated from Emily, who was squeezed among several male admirers. Manfred was on another table with his new friends, the paper readers and the silent girls; in order to fit, everyone grouped themselves to be three people to one side of each table. The men were sopping wet and dripped over the benches. The water also fell on Manfred's shorts and over the paper plates and napkins.

The boy managed to cater for the entire boat from his makeshift kitchen, even though there must have been forty or fifty people aboard. Kem and the boy, whose face was blackened, served the lunches quickly and unceremoniously. They handed round bottles of tomato ketchup, which struck Manfred as incongruous, and everyone ate their meals enthusiastically, loudly and sweatily.

There was no room for Manfred's knees or elbows and he tried to use his plastic knife and fork with his arms by his sides. The plastic bent and crumpled uselessly against the meat. Manfred looked at his watch; it was nearly eleven o'clock and they had left at seven thirty.

He gave up on the cutlery and picked up the chicken and salad in his hands. The chicken was bright pink inside, but Manfred was so hungry that he ate it quickly; he doubted they would be able to get any more food until they were home. No one else seemed bothered by the pink meat, least of all Emily who was eating enthusiastically, laughing frequently and getting tomato sauce over her mouth as the men said things that Manfred could not hear in sly, eye-rolling undertones. Manfred felt a pang of jealousy and wished he could be sitting next to her. Even if they did not say anything to each other; he would be more comfortable if he could feel her leg rub against his, instead of the hairy leg that was rubbing up and down against him at that moment.

'What part of the trip are you most looking forward to?' he

asked, fed up with being looked at and rebelliously thinking, if Emily can engage them in conversation then so can I.

The men looked at him blankly and the girls, who had been so relaxed in the sea with Emily, ignored him. They ate their food carefully and methodically. Unbowed, Manfred tried again, miming words where he could and making an effort to communicate. They made an effort to reply.

'Relaxing,' said one. 'Doing nothing,' added the second, 'doing nothing in water. What you looking forward to?'

'Oh, the turtle beach, definitely,' Manfred replied.

'Yes, me too,' said the second one, which struck Manfred as a bit odd considering that she had just claimed that not doing anything was her main interest. Crawling across sand and inching towards nesting turtles protecting their eggs was hardly doing nothing. This was the scenario Manfred envisaged for the afternoon and which kept him going.

After lunch Kem gave a little speech about what they could expect to see for the rest of the day. This evolved almost immediately into a more general talk. 'We are trying very hard to be part of the European Union,' he explained, and the audience nodded and digested. Manfred thought that if he lived here, the last thing he would want would be to become part of Europe. But it was economic, he supposed. He remembered the waiter in the restaurant looking at his sterling notes.

The Germans ran back upstairs and reclaimed their sun beds. Manfred stayed where he was. Gradually the boat moved out from the shelter of the bay and continued its slow, inexorable way along the coastline.

The sea was endless, a sheer blue sheet like hammered steel, stretching out to the horizon where it met a solid block of blue marble sky. Manfred cupped his head in his hand, leant his elbow on the rough wooden rim of the boat, and watched the horizon slowly move up and down in time with the gulet's creaking. The spectacular scenery on the near side had become dull now. It looked the same as it did half an hour ago, only shifted a bit to the left. No matter how beautiful something is, he thought, it becomes tedious if you experience it for too long. Surely they would be there soon. They were heading towards another bay, so perhaps this was where the journey ended.

A gangly man with a camera went round the boat and took pictures of everyone. Emily smiled sweetly and the photographer spent extra time over getting her photo right, asking her to sit forward a bit, or push her hair back, or look out to sea. Manfred scowled at him for his picture, which the man took briefly and without comment. The gulet pulled up at a deserted beach and the camera man leapt off and disappeared into the sand. Manfred thought that they had arrived.

'Now we get into the small boat,' announced Kem, 'as we are unable to take the large boat up the delta.' Everyone trooped out of the gulet and down the narrow gangplank which bowed and wheezed beneath each passenger. Larger, faster and sweatier people pushed past Manfred and he was left till last, like a marble being forced down different directions in a wooden toy. He regressed for a moment to a child at play school, forever left behind by big children. He waited until the last of the crowd had bustled off the boat and then stepped gingerly down the gangplank, which barely moved under his weight.

The Germans jumped onto the small boat. By the time Manfred got inside, all the seats with cushions had been taken and Manfred had to sit against a metal pole. Emily tried to save a seat for him but she was quickly swamped by men keen to sit next to her, who pretended not to understand her hand gestures and excited babble and squeezed up tightly against her. There was no room for manoeuvre because the boat only had enough seats for everyone to sit tightly packed against everyone else.

The metal pole Manfred was leaning against had a small metal chuck sticking into the base of his neck. The air was a mixture of sweat, cheap perfume, beer and diesel. He could not sit forward because the seat was bowed in the middle and it strained his back. Nor could he get his neck above or below the piece of metal or manipulate himself into any position where it was comfortable.

He tried to sit cross-legged but the man on his right smacked his knees with an 'aiieee' sound and glared at him until he moved his legs. Manfred contemplated sitting in the pit of the boat, but it sloshed with water. As the boat set off, the gentle motion nudged the metal chuck into Manfred's neck every few seconds. He tried to angle himself sideways against the pole but the person next to him on the other side kept pushing him back on to it with every movement of the boat. The sun was fierce and unforgiving now.

He concentrated on two of the fat German women in order to ignore the pain. After about half an hour they exploded in a raucous cacophony of laughter about something or other. He looked over at Emily, who was sitting opposite him, crammed between two of the enthusiastic men who had adopted her on the main boat and seemed to be permanently attached to her.

Emily did not find their company entertaining any more. They frequently rubbed themselves against her, exaggerating the motion of the boat to imply it was the motion that was causing the contact. They had hands that were always hovering in front of her breast whenever she leant forward. On the numerous occasions they made contact they withdrew from her slowly, full of apology. She watched Manfred silently, wondering what he was looking so gloomy about.

The backs of her thighs were itching and she moved her buttocks up and down on the bench, trying to get comfortable. Two men watched her, not blinking till their eyes watered. She closed her eyes and found herself back in her office, sifting paperwork. It was the most boring, hateful part of the day, and the part she had most looked forward to being able to forget about for the two weeks of the honeymoon. She found the image soothing, and she longed to be sitting at her quiet desk, on her own, in a room that did not move up and down, where she did not feel tired and hungry, and where she had a comfortable chair and space to breathe.

Emily put her sunglasses on. Most people had hidden themselves behind glasses by now and Manfred felt distanced from everyone on the boat, especially Emily. This made him anxious. He realised he had barely spoken to her since they left the harbour.

He considered this. It was not right for a newly married couple. What had he done wrong, he thought nervously; why did he not feel comfortable? Should he be more assertive and address the situation, or would it be stronger to accept things the way there were, and know that when they arrived wherever they were supposed to arrive, they would be together again? He frowned. He would talk to her when they were on dry land and explain how he felt.

On the other hand perhaps it was normal. He did not know; he watched her. Her expression was impenetrable.

He was distracted as they sailed slowly and silently down through the rushes by a magical feeling of anticipation. He was excited, but also calm; he was floating along with the boat; moving, but still.

There was a flurry of excitement; a turtle was spotted in the rushes. Kem switched the engine off and drew the boat to a slow lull, letting it float along where the gentle tide took it.

For a while, the passengers looked out with a sense of intoxication, but saw nothing. Kem turned the boat round and drove back, in an attempt to find the turtle. After a while it emerged from the water again. It was large and black and looked like a vast tractor hub floating at the side of the water. It did not move, but clung to the bank with the waves created by the boat lapping against its shell, as if it was scared to stay in the water but too frightened to venture on to the land.

The contents of the boat watched it for several minutes. Manfred found it uninteresting, then disliked himself for thinking this. Considering how far they had come to see it, he thought it might at least do something a bit more spectacular, such as swim. But everyone else seemed quite content, gasping at it in wonder and frenetically taking photographs. What should have been a quiet moment was like being surrounded by a plague of crickets.

Emily, entranced, took her camera out and wound the film on without once taking her eyes off the turtle. He heard her breathing heavily. 'Isn't it wonderful?'

'Mmm,' he agreed, feeling that to deserve this status it should make a noise or lay an egg or something. The turtle clung to the side of the rock, motionless.

'Are you sure it's not dead?' he asked, after they'd all studied it for several minutes.

'Of course it's not dead,' Emily muttered. After it had continued resolutely not to move for several minutes, she bit her lip. 'At least... I don't think so...'

The boat drifted on and eventually hit the shore a hundred yards or so downstream. Kem noisily explained in three languages that they had just witnessed a caretta carettas turtle. Looking back, the turtle had vanished. 'Oh good,' Emily said. 'That means it wasn't dead.'

'Yes. Unless it just sank.' Manfred held a hand up vertically and slid it down the palm of his other hand, to illustrate how this could have occurred. Emily pouted.

Four hours since they had begun the journey they turned a bend in the canal. Kem announced that in a moment they would see the tombs. The boat heaved and rolled as everyone leapt up. It adjusted well to this unexpected redistribution of weight, particularly with regard to those members of the party who had the most weight to redistribute. Everyone gathered along the left-hand rail with their cameras. Manfred tried to see through the mass of heads and flab but saw nothing of the tombs.

He took the opportunity to sit on a cushion. It took a long time for the boat to weave its way through the reeds and follow the lazy path of the river, which took the path of least resistance between the tightly growing greenery. The reeds were as high as the boat and the passengers could only glimpse the tombs, high in the mountainside above them.

After a couple of minutes and fifty or sixty rolls of film, most got bored with jostling for the best view and pointing and photographing, and sat down again. When Manfred noticed the burly, angry looking man whom he had previously sat next to, waddling towards him, he got up and walked quickly to the front of the boat.

He had an uninterrupted view of the tombs as the boat got closer to them and they came fully into view. The reeds still flickered up occasionally, obscuring the tombs as the boat moved slowly and silently past. Without the background music of excited babble and cameras clicking away, it was a magical sight. The tombs were cut directly from the rock. Resembling stone houses with pediments and pillars, they were like sculptures hewn directly from the rock itself. They were awe-inspiring, like a set for a film.

Manfred noticed Kem standing beside him. 'It would be nice if we could get up there and actually, you know, explore them.'

Kem shrugged. 'Well yes, you can get up, if you are, you know, the mountain goat.' He looked Manfred up and down.

'Much easier for you to stay on the boat and relax.'

Emily, squashed amongst the hordes of sweaty, smelly bodies, found that she was able to secrete herself into a corner by a slow process of shifting and nudging her way along the bench. The bodies shifted around her like bacteria moving slowly in a circle. She sat contentedly and pulled her guidebook out of her bag.

Way up in the mountains, Manfred saw a pale man of about sixty in a baseball cap and shorts inspecting the tombs. He doesn't look like a mountain goat, thought Manfred, as the boat slid slowly past. It had taken four hours to get here and as he thought this, the tombs disappeared from sight.

Manfred sat back in the boat. The metal pole and joint dug into him. The boat turned a corner and he winced as the full glare of the hot and angry sun hit him. Manfred closed his eyes. He tried to lean sideways, but there was no room on the seat between him and the fat man he was stuffed up against. Four more hours of this to get back home, he thought. He should be enjoying it, he told himself; this was an adventure, it was living, it was life. But he felt tired and irritable and wanted to go home.

You're just tired, he told himself as he closed his eyes. When he was at home and comfortable, he would look back and want to be here again; he would want to be seeing the turtle and the tombs, and it would have been worth it.

He must have dozed for a few moments, because when he opened his eyes his head was resting against Emily's forehead. She rubbed his back gently. He blinked, disoriented, wondering how everyone had shifted round and Emily was beside him. He looked around vaguely and wondered how much time had gone past. The tombs had disappeared. Kem was rushing round offering beer. A posh couple asked for two glasses of port. Kem asked them what port was.

'You speak to him,' the posh woman said wearily to her husband. 'You're the one who can communicate with them.'

Manfred looked around; the scenery was different too. The tall reeds had disappeared and the river was wider. There were trees dangling into the water, stretching huge, gnarled branches like overlapping snakes into the green stillness. There was a distant sound of insects and unfamiliar birds.

Was this a mangrove swamp, Manfred wondered. He did not know what a mangrove was. Are the trees dangling into the water the mangroves, or is the mangrove the area, like other groves?

A village was visible through the overhanging trees. People gathered loosely along the waterfront. They gazed boldly at the boat, curious but unsmiling. A man, naked but for a scarf roughly tied round his legs, sawed planks of wood. They fell from the sawing horse and stuck upended into the thick mud.

Inside a loosely constructed garage made from sheets of corrugated plastic, the wreck of a fishing boat sloped drunkenly on its underbelly like a stranded whale, its rudder poking feebly out from underneath and sticking into the earth. The boat's blue paint was bleached and worn away to the yellow paint underneath, which in turn was worn away to reveal pale yellowish wood. Holes had begun to appear in the bulging sides of the boat, and the struts emerged like broken ribs or snapped fingers, clawing hopelessly from the dark interior.

The little boat travelled another half mile upstream, and drew up alongside some cliffs on the other side of the village. It floated along for another hundred feet or so, then the cliffs dropped away and the flat pool of the bay became visible. Its tide was so low against the lip of the beach that it created thousands of tiny lakes in the vast extent of the beach, before the land finally lifted upwards and the beach proper began. The Germans crowded to the front of the boat and leapt off, and the boat swayed up and down against the network of planks and rough walkways that traversed the no man's land between sand and water.

III

'So this is the turtle beach.'

'What's the matter?' asked Emily.

Manfred looked out at the heaving mass of bodies and coconut umbrellas and the raffia tent with hundreds of people underneath it, all sat at matting tables or heaped around the bar. He stomped off to find Kem, leaving Emily chewing her finger.

'This is the turtle beach?' he asked incredulously.

'Yes,' said Kem. 'At certain times of the year, the turtles come to this beach and lay their eggs. It is a very famous spot.'

'And the rest of the time, it's…?' Manfred waved his hands around.

Kem shrugged. 'At the moment, as you can see, it is a beautiful beach. People are enjoying themselves. Relax, enjoy yourself.'

Manfred nodded. Kem was right. The beach was packed with sunbathing tourists, all having a fabulous time.

'There aren't any turtles at the moment?'

'No, not at this time of year.'

'But we came here because we wanted to see turtles.'

Kem shrugged. 'When the turtles are here, the beach is closed off to people to protect them.'

Manfred looked at him mutinously. Kem spread his arms wide. 'You are on the beach now. We are all here to sunbathe on turtle beach – something to tell your friends, yes? Enjoy yourself, relax.' He slapped Manfred on the back and wandered off.

Emily removed her more unnecessary articles of clothing. When Manfred saw her in her bikini again he felt a familiar swelling of pride and an equally familiar one of excitement. He liked the fact that she did not seem to realise how attractive she was. Whenever he tentatively tried to tell her, she would giggle and blush; sometimes she would become coy if she were naked in front of him. Although, remembering that morning, maybe she was becoming less shy. Being in a hot country was liberating her.

'We're here for two and a half hours apparently,' said Emily quietly. They looked across to the fat German women, unconcernedly cooking themselves in the coffin-sized plots of beach they had somehow secured. The beach was a heaving mass of multicoloured bodies, and there was no shade to be seen. Sweat broke out out on Manfred's spine and in the pit of his stomach. He shivered.

'What are we going to do here for two and a half hours?' Manfred said, trying to stay calm. 'That means we won't get back till… something like nine o'clock tonight.'

Emily bit her lip. The only visible shade was under a kind of shack constructed of bamboo poles and a coconut matting roof, which was evidently the restaurant.

'I'm really hungry,' Emily said, looking at it. Manfred nodded. 'We'll see if we can get some food,' he said, trying to deal robustly with the situation and be stoical instead of crumpling up and thumping the ground, which was what he felt like doing. They walked towards the restaurant, the sand like hot couscous under their feet.

But the restaurant was as packed as the beach; the tables were crammed full, the spaces between the tables were occupied by people trying to move between the tables, there was no pathway to the long queue that wound round the bar, and people were spilling out onto the edge of the beach, trying to stay in the shadow of the roof. Even if they could get a table, which was unlikely, it would be an uncomfortable experience.

Manfred walked briskly to the toilet, ignoring the sign that asked for 500,000 for the privilege. When he came back Emily was thoughtfully rubbing sun cream into her arm and staring out to sea. Manfred concentrated on her slim stomach moving almost imperceptibly up and down. He put his arm round her. 'Don't worry,' he said, trying to instil confidence that he did not feel himself.

Some distance from the toilet, a man with a face like a walnut sold bottles of water from a bucket. The bottles bobbed in ice-cold water and the man occasionally dipped his dirty hand in and flicked cold water over passers-by to tempt them. Manfred glanced at Emily and the same thought ran through their heads. On any other occasion, they would have not gone anywhere near the man and his water; Manfred suspected that the bottles had been filled up from a tap, and was not the mineral water it claimed to be on the label.

He asked the man how much they were. He wanted a million for each two litre bottle, which was an outrageous mark-up compared to how much they were sold for in supermarkets; but Manfred bought two. The man grinned, his puckered face creasing so much that his eyes became points of light and then disappeared into the folds of his cheeks. He opened his mouth in a parody of a smile, one gold tooth clinging on where organic teeth had decayed to stumps long ago.

They walked along the length of the beach, searching for shade. Whitened twigs and the fuzz of dry greenery was all that could survive in the harsh environment. There were occasional patches of green on sand dunes, but these oases were all occupied with people who had also gone looking for shade.

'If we carry on far enough,' reasoned Emily, 'there should be somewhere that's empty. After a certain point, people always give up.'

Manfred nodded. 'We've got enough time, after all,' he said as he followed her. After five or ten minutes, they had found nothing. Emily walked at the water's edge, letting it lap at her toes. The slope of the beach was so shallow that she could walk ten feet or so into the water and her feet were still barely covered.

'Come for a swim with me,' she whispered enticingly.

He shook his head. She tugged at his arm. 'Come on,' she said. 'Come and swim.' She kissed him gently on his ear. He looked at her. 'Really,' he said, trying to smile, 'really, I can't.'

She walked quickly down to the water, hiding her face behind her hair. She swam vigorously to the far edge. She saw for the first time how moody he was, and did not understand why she did not seem to be able to do anything about it. She could not imagine why he would not come and swim; he did not even seem to want to splash around in the water. That was all she wanted; it was not as if she was challenging him to a race.

He watched her swimming furiously and energetically and felt ashamed. When she emerged, he looked at her with a pale, nervous face, expecting her to be angry with him. She walked confidently along the great distance of shallow water, her toned thighs flexing and reflexing as she paced up towards him. She used her sarong to dry the excess water from her hair, knowing the rest would quickly dry in the overhead sun. She hugged Manfred and kissed him, enveloping him in her arms so fiercely he was reminded of his father.

They walked another long distance along the beach, still unable to find shade. 'I'm really hot,' Emily said unhappily, a point of frustration breaking out on her forehead, casting unfamiliar lines across her face. Ahead of them the bay curved round like the underside of orange peel. The mountains that emerged on the far side were temptingly green and the beach in front of the mountains was sheltered by shade – this beach was deserted.

Emily glanced at Manfred and they picked up speed. But it was so far away, Manfred wondered if they would ever get there before it was time to start walking back again.

'At least we've got water,' Emily said. They knelt on the sand and Manfred opened the first bottle; it was like champagne after a long sweaty sports match. As Manfred had suspected, the seal on the cap was broken. They would just have to hope the water was safe. Emily took a long, sensuous draught and Manfred watched the delicate ridge in her neck move in and out rhythmically.

He drank a similar amount and glanced at the bottle; the first half had gone. He felt his knees glowing, burning slightly on the sand, and he felt like lying down and closing his eyes.

They kept walking, but still found no shade and the empty beach did not get any closer. They listened to the sound of their own breath, audible against the silent, hot air.

'I'm a bit bored', said Emily uncertainly, as if she didn't think she could or should be bored on her honeymoon and was unsure whether to admit it. She looked at her watch. 'And it's so hot,' she added, as if he might have forgotten. She was perspiring on her temples and neck. He had not seen her sweat before. She looked fragile and beautiful. She had also acquired, in the last two days, a deep, smooth tan; he felt pale and unattractive in comparison.

'It's a ridiculous time to come here,' she complained, 'just when it's the hottest part of the day. And why do we have to be here for so long? And why didn't they tell us we would be here this long?'

He had not seen her get upset like this. She was usually the calm, encouraging one, who let him complain about something, and then told him everything would be all right and gave him confidence. She never took much notice of his grumbling and he never meant much by it; he was just a person who needed to get things off his chest and be reassured. They complemented each other well for this reason. Anyone other than Emily would find Manfred irritable and negative and anyone other than Manfred would find Emily lifeless and dull. At least, this was what Manfred thought. Now that her lip was protruding like a child about to cry, and she appeared frustrated, he was disoriented and did not know how to deal with it.

'Well,' he said, trying to think what she would say to him in a situation like this, 'it'll be all right.'

'Yes, I know,' she said, reverting immediately to her quiet way of speaking and letting her hands hover over her lap as they walked. 'I just want to go home.' She was tired and hungry. Perhaps when they walked back, she thought, the restaurant would not be so full.

There was one more dune with some green on it but it was impenetrable; there was no one there, but it was covered in bracken and thistle. The sand was dirty, covered in plastic bottles and the remains of a fire.

Manfred saw a waterfall, with bright blue water trickling down onto a carpet of green shoots. He could even hear it. But as they walked further forward, it resolved itself into a narrow strip of rock, suggesting flowing water because the rock was blue and jagged, and the green shoots at the bottom were patches of the usual lifeless, bracken-like dried out greenery. And the sound that he thought was water was the humming sound of the air; he could hear it now that he listened, but had not noticed it before.

Eventually they reached the extremity of the beach, where a small inlet of water separated them from a rocky promontory. Several people at the water's edge took their shoes and socks off and waded out, laughing as the water suddenly leapt up to their middles and they had to swim across. Fifty feet or so away was the other beach, with its long stretch of shadow. Manfred shuddered as he watched them swimming, imagining the sand slipping away under his feet and leaving him struggling in water.

Emily frowned. 'That's quite dangerous,' she murmured, 'there could be whirlpools in the middle.' Manfred did not know how she could tell, but was pleased she said it; it meant she would not want to go in.

Emily watched the swimmers with concern, but they reached the other side safely and rested in their hard-earned shade. She looked at Manfred with pursed lips. 'I'm not going in,' he said, folding his arms. She nodded. Ahead of them, the beach ran out and the landscape became sheer rock face with water gently lapping against it. 'And I'm not mountaineering either,' he added, as they looked up at it. She grinned.

They turned back. After ten minutes or so, Emily gripped Manfred's arm. There was a small patch of green, and no one underneath it. Walking towards it, they saw sun-bleached branches in the bush, with more dead branches scattered on the sand, but no bottles or litter. 'How did we miss this last time?' murmured Emily, as she laid her sarong across the sand and pushed some twigs out of the way.

'Perhaps there were people here and now they've gone,' Manfred suggested. Or it's another mirage, he thought. But if so it was a very durable one because they were able to climb inside it. Manfred lay down next to Emily with a groan of relief. It was cool and dark in the little alcove, which was created by branches suspended over the sand. Emily put her head on his chest. They looked up into the green canopy with wide eyes. It was the first time they had been able to open their eyes properly all day, and they took great pleasure in it, pulling faces and staring as wide-eyed as they could until they looked at each other and laughed.

While Manfred closed his eyes, Emily crawled through the bushes. It was relatively easy to get through because the greenery stopped a foot or so above the ground and most of the branches supposedly supporting it were dead, apparently calcified, and could be pushed to one side.

She found herself looking into a small lagoon, cut off on three sides by sandbanks and connected to the beach by a narrow strip of sand. Overhanging greenery put the lagoon in shade. Emily lay on her front on the sand and looked into the water. An unmoving reflection of her stared back. She looked into her eyes. She touched her face, pulling at her skin, to see what it looked like in the reflection. She leant forward and brought her face close to the surface of the water. She put her tongue out and licked the reflection. Immediately it broke up and vanished.

'Emily.'

She leapt up. 'You startled me.'

'Sorry. What are you doing?'

'The water here is very clean. It's why the turtles come here. So I decided to taste it. And then I thought, bad idea. The tourists probably all piss in it.'

Manfred looked at her bronzed thighs and the slight imprint of hair pressing against her bikini pants. Impelled, he knelt in front of her and gently kissed her in the triangle of cloth. She knelt down with him, pushing herself away, embarrassed.

The listened to the crickets and lazily ran their hands over each other's bodies. Manfred looked at his watch; they still had nearly an hour to kill. Just as he felt himself slowly starting to doze, Emily ran a hand over his shorts and burrowed into them like a small mammal. Manfred wriggled to begin with, then groaned in enjoyment.

IV

Emily looked at her watch. 'Oh God.'

'What is it?'

She was breathing deeply, almost hyperventilating. She got to her feet and snatched her sarong and bag from the ground. The sarong was covered in sand, which scattered in his face as he ran after her, bending down to pick up the second bottle of water and crawl through the canopy of green. 'It's been three hours,' she called, as he followed her out. They ran across the sand, both realising with a gut-wrenching pang that if the boat had gone without them they would be stranded. They had no idea where the nearest town was, or when they would be able to get another boat from the beach; presumably not until the next day. There was no guarantee there would be anywhere to stay in the village. They didn't even know if there was any way to reach the village by land, if there was no boat to take them through the reeds.

When they saw the canopy of the restaurant, they slowed down. The Germans were still sunbathing and Kem was trying to round them up, telling them the boat would soon be leaving. Manfred and Emily ground to a halt in the sand. Kem and the boy who had cooked lunch looked at them in surprise. Emily and Manfred stood still, panting, looking at Kem and unable to speak. Reluctantly the Germans, red and puffing like boiled lobsters, uprighted themselves in the sand.

'I'm glad we were late,' murmured Emily eventually as they stood with their hands on their knees and felt their chests hammering. 'Imagine if we'd come back and had to sit here waiting.'

Manfred nodded, too busy drinking the rest of the water to reply.

Kem and the boy, who according to Emily was called Ali, were still persuading the German men to come back to the boat. Manfred gave the restaurant another try. It was still full; making his way past the shoal of bodies that lay heaped up against the entrance, Manfred could see that even if he had time to queue, there was nothing portable that he could take away. 'I'm absolutely starving,' Emily said. 'I think I'm going to faint if we don't eat something soon.'

'Perhaps he'll have something on the boat,' said Manfred doubtfully, not expecting this to be the case for a moment. He felt very relieved that he had forced himself to eat the chicken earlier. The small boat bobbed in the lapping water as they walked towards it, then it bounced up and down as they climbed aboard.

Manfred flicked through Emily's battered guidebook. Downstream of the beach was another village, full of ancient architecture and beautiful, steep rocky pathways that led to spectacular views over the lagoons and the reed marshes. According to the book it was the 'must-see' of the trip: orange trees, sleepy whitewashed houses and churches nestling amongst the ancient fortifications and excavations.

Emily showed the page to Kem. 'Do we go here?' she asked, her eyes lighting up. She forgot all about the beach fiasco.

Kem looked at the pictures and the description, pushing his sunglasses back on his nose like an old woman peering at a crossword. 'Unfortunately not,' he eventually announced.

'Why not?'

'It takes a while to walk there.'

'Ten minutes, it says in the book.'

'Well…' Kem said. 'Only old people are interested, I am afraid.'

'We're interested.'

Kem shrugged and lengthened his mouth sympathetically.

Emily nodded. 'That's a shame.'

'Can't you make a special exception for us?' Manfred asked. 'Under the circumstances.'

'Well,' Kem said, looking at his watch, 'unfortunately we do not have time now anyway. We have to get back. The other passengers want to go home, it has been a long day,' he said apologetically. 'I am sorry. I have to do what everyone wants.' He spread his hands wide.

'Well,' said Manfred, sensing that he was going to snap and wasn't going to be able to help it, and knowing he would regret it afterwards, 'perhaps if we had not spent so many hours sat on the beach doing nothing, there would have been time.'

'Perhaps there would,' Kem agreed quietly. He walked stiffly away.

Emily, less tired and irritable than Manfred, bit her lip. Manfred was right, but Kem was right as well. It was not Kem's fault if most of the people he took on tours want to sit on beaches and go swimming. But she understood Manfred's frustration. There were so many wonderful places along this stretch of coastline and they had wasted the whole day and were now sailing straight past them; she had the sense of something being lost forever, knowing she would never come back.

For the rest of the honeymoon, she resolved, they would not go on any tours but would make their own way and go to see what they wanted to see. They had had their baptism now; they did not have to go on organised trips. But Manfred had been unfair. She would take Kem to one side at a quiet moment and apologise to him. Having decided this, she felt better. She realised that she would probably not stick to her decision, but tried to ignore this thought when it popped into her head.

Manfred avoided looking at Emily. The boat sailed slowly and silently through the reeds. After about twenty minutes, it pulled up at the edge of the beach where the larger boat was moored.

'I think this is the far side of where we got to,' said Emily, as they crossed the network of creaking wooden slats and bridges. Manfred looked across to the flat expanse of beach and the shallow incline to the water, and the shape of the mountain behind the beach, and nodded slowly. 'Yes,' he said, 'we walked all the way up here.'

'We could have just stayed there; if we'd walked a little further we'd have got here.'

Manfred nodded. There was a free for all as lots of red, desiccated bodies made a dash to get the best seats on top. The boat rocked wildly as all along its side, the Germans heaved and flailed. They grabbed hold of the other boat as soon as it was within reach and flung themselves aboard like overweight salmon struggling upstream. Some of them fell into the pit of the boat and lay there like stranded whales, laughing uncontrollably, before breathlessly pulling themselves upright and making a dash for the staircase. Manfred tried to stay vertical amidst the smaller boat's drunken rocking. He shook his head resignedly at Emily, who put a hand over her mouth and giggled.

Everyone else was aboard and Emily and Manfred were the only ones left. 'Come, come,' said Kem as Manfred failed to orient himself against the swaying beams of the gulet, which moved and bumped against the smaller boat at entirely different times and angles to the smaller boat's movements. Manfred found it impossible to work out when the boats would be at a conjunction he could navigate, and smacked elbows and knees against the wood when he miscalculated.

Gradually the boats started to separate and Manfred panicked for a moment as he looked down and saw a narrow strip of bright green water beneath him. He slipped forward and fell into the boat. Once back on his feet, he pushed himself up against the side and helped a nervous Emily aboard, grasping both of her hands and pulling her on top of him, her feet dangling behind her and slipping on the rims of both boats.

The boat chugged slowly away from the sand and travelled down a shallow channel between two strips of beach. Ahead of them, another boat had stopped moving. There was some kind of commotion aboard. As he looked across, Kem laughed softly to himself with a guttural wheeze like a cold car starting. Ali hooted and pointed at the boat, shaking his head and slapping his hand on his leg.

The boat was listing in the water and several people jumped off. Someone threw a rope towards them and they lined themselves up along this rope until they were strung out like buoys. Those still on board shouted and waved. In front of the low sun, the people up to their hips in the shallow water were silhouettes, leaning to one side as they pulled at the rope. The boat, ignoring their efforts, listed further.

Slowly and smugly, Manfred and Emily's gulet sailed past. They watched as another boat pulled alongside to help; then that got stuck too. The sun was still powerful and unforgiving. Black shapes pushed and pulled futilely; then swam round to the other side to try again.

Manfred scratched the back of his neck and Emily bit her lip. Most people in the boat found it funny; pointing and laughing like children seeing another child suffering. 'I'm glad we're not in that one,' Emily murmured.

Kem hurried to the front of the gulet to supervise the navigation. Arguing volubly with Ali the whole time, both energetically throwing their arms around and shaking their heads, they plotted a course some distance from the two stranded boats but not too close to the beach on the other side, and maintained a slow, steady speed. The boat turned slightly, shuddered, then stalled and stopped.

'Perhaps he's thinking about it,' Emily said, to fill the sudden silence. 'Perhaps there's another way.' An ominous hush fell over the boat. The posh woman sat with her head elegantly balanced on her hand, smoking a cigarette. Two German women sat quietly like rodents hearing a storm and trying to stay still in their cage. Their faces settled into the folds of their chins and their arms became lost in the voluminous folds of their laps.

The engine started up again hopefully, and everyone twitched and fiddled with their hands as if on a runway, waiting for take-off. The engine chugged for several minutes without the boat moving, then it died away again. Somebody coughed. There was the excited chattering of voices arguing. The argument became heated as something was dropped, or thrown, or slammed.

Finally, a beaming Kem emerged to rally the troops, clapping his hands and emanating confidence. He laughed and joked and told everyone not to worry, then clapped again for attention. Everyone docilely turned to listen, looking at him like children expecting leadership on a school trip, so devoid of energy after the long hungry day that they were pleased that any thinking would be done by someone else.

'Okay, what we are going to do,' said Kem, 'all the men in the boat, are going to get out. Then when weight has dropped, boat will be able to travel until in its depth again. Then we travel round the edge of the bay, and the men will walk across the sand and meet the boat on the other side, where it will be okay to get into boat again.' After this announcement, Kem quickly disappeared.

Manfred felt a plunging feeling. He went to find Kem or Ali and explain to them that he could not swim, but they were running round organising people and fetching ropes and poles, and he could not attract anyone's attention.

Emily smiled as he found his way back, thinking he was going to follow the others. But he sat down next to her and put his hands on his knees. She pursed her lips, wondering why he had such a determined, set expression on his face. At the side of the boat, men were jumping off into the water, which was no more than knee high; it was no wonder the boat had grounded.

Fat women clasped their husbands to their bosoms and murmured fast, incomprehensible messages to them, before waving them off as if they were soldiers going to war. Each one stood astride the rim of the boat, bold and proud with the sun behind him, and looked back at his loved one before leaping off and out of sight.

I'm not going, thought Manfred firmly, leaning his head forward and feeling his mind knot up against the idea. They can say what they like, he thought, I'm not going. Ahead, he saw Ali waving at him, pushing his arms to the side of the boat to indicate to Manfred that that was where he had to go. Manfred pretended not to have seen him.

Emily opened her mouth to talk to Manfred, then closed it again. Could he just not be bothered? Was he so fed up with the day that he had decided he wanted no further part of it? Perhaps she should offer to go herself, she thought, chewing the inside of her mouth, racked with indecision. She didn't mind going at all. But they were in a different country, she told herself, they do things differently here. The men do one thing and the women do another. She might be committing some cultural mistake if she said she would go. Or she might be seen to be usurping his maleness. She looked at him uncomfortably.

'Everyone else is going,' she murmured, touching his arm. 'Well I'm not,' he said, more savagely than he intended. She recoiled instinctively from him. He looked up and tried to make eye contact with her, to apologise for speaking sharply, but she had turned her head away from him and was watching the line of men walking across the sand. He lifted his arm to put his hand on her leg, then thought better of it. He shook his head; he was too tired to think straight about what to do. He couldn't go but he couldn't stay; and he didn't feel able to admit to her why he couldn't go. It was too late for that; she would just look at him in amazement.

Emily looked round. Two of the other women were looking at her strangely, glancing at Manfred then back to her. One of them, who had a big wart, appeared to leer, but Emily, giving her the benefit of the doubt, decided that she was squinting in the light and it only looked like a leer because she was so ugly.

Manfred jumped to his feet. He found Kem in the little cabin at the front of the boat, and insisted on speaking to him. Kem glanced up at him and his brow furrowed. 'You follow the men, yes,' he said, turning back to the sprawling mass of ropes, cables and metal buckles and equipment that lay in a jumbled heap at his feet. He put his hands on his knees and bent over and peered at it, his head shaking slightly.

'No,' said Manfred.

'What?' said Kem, not turning round.

'I'm sorry, I can't swim.'

Kem straightened up, turned to him and frowned, then grinned. Manfred watched the gold tooth glinting. For the first time, Kem took his sunglasses off. He put his hand on Manfred's shoulder. 'You do not need to swim,' he said. 'You only need to walk across the beach and then wade to the boat.'

Manfred looked into his eyes as if mesmerised. 'It will not get higher than here.' Kem bent down and tapped his hand across Manfred's knee. 'At the very most. Okay? Now you go.' He turned back to his cables. Ali, standing by uselessly, scratched his head.

Manfred, too tired to argue, turned and made his way back to Emily. He was unconvinced by what Kem said but incapable of making a decision, and could not think clearly enough to know what kind of decision he was making by going. His half-awake mind just wanted to take the easiest option, which was to follow everyone else.

Emily was sitting some distance from the other women, reading her guidebook. Curled up on the seat, she looked tiny and fragile and not quite real; a three-quarter size version of his new wife. She glanced up when she heard him coming. He looked uncertainly at her and she looked uncertainly back.

'Well,' he said shortly, 'I'm off then.'

She dropped her book without bothering to keep it on its page, and hugged him. Behind him she could see the women stirring and watching curiously to see what would happen.

'Well,' he said, 'see you later then.'

She nodded and kissed him. She didn't know why he was making such a big drama of it, but everything felt so intense, and the fact that people were watching his every move meant she thought that he felt as if he were living out some drama, playing a part in some performance. He climbed off the window ledge and fell clumsily in the water. A sharp jab of pain ran through his ankle. When he looked back, Emily was thumbing through her guide book, trying to find the page.

Manfred waded through the shallow water and onto the bank of sand. He ran across the sand to catch up with the others, but realised when he came over the brow of the dunes that he needn't have rushed. Everyone was walking so slowly that they were only three or four hundred feet ahead of him. Some had already reached the water's edge and were standing with their feet in water, looking around as if not sure in which direction to go. The slower, fatter ones trailed behind, looking around at the mountains or picking up pebbles and tossing them into the water.

Manfred looked back at the boat. Ali and Kem were up to their waists in the water, carrying a rope across to the line of men standing alongside the other boat. From the mime that was being carried out in silhouette against the ever-present sun, now huge and red in the lower quarter of the sky, Manfred guessed that the men were being coaxed into rescuing their second stranded ship of the afternoon. Kem waded back to the boat, all the time waving his arms enthusiastically and shouting encouragement.

Manfred caught up with the fattest of the party and avoided making eye contact with him. The last thing he wanted was to be forced into a conversation with no chance of escaping for half an hour. Those at the front had worked out the direction in which they needed to walk along the beach. The sandbank continued in a long, curling spit into the centre of the bay, and then dropped sharply away into the water. This, presumably, was where the boat would collect them; it could pull alongside here without getting stuck.

Looking to his right, he could see that the boat was now upright. By standing still and concentrating on the scenery behind the boat, he could tell that it had started moving. A breeze came as if by magic from the still air and rippled the back of his T-shirt. He closed his eyes and listened to the unfamiliar sound. After a few seconds, it faded away and the beach was still and silent again.

The boat rounded the far edge of the spit, keeping its distance to ensure it did not ground again. Ahead of Manfred, a long line of men continued along the spit, suspended now between two glittering blades of water. The sand curled and disappeared like the yellow brick road. Manfred looked at the water enveloping him now on both sides and felt a nervousness in his stomach like an itch under a scab. He ignored it, and concentrated on the moving black blob that was the boat.

To his left, beyond the gently moving sea, was the mountainside with its reddish clumps of sand and occasional flowerings of green scrub. Manfred saw the patterns of the mountain and the leaves of the plants with great clarity; his eyesight seemed better than it usually was and he could make out much detail on the mountainside, these details bright and full of energy and buzzing against each other like air shimmering in heat. He felt that he was *looking* at the mountain for the first time, as opposed to just seeing it. It was an image that imprinted itself on his mind for the rest of the long, portentous walk towards the boat.

The boat swung round and hovered ahead of them in the bay. It was a large blueish shadow now, not quite opaque because he could see small windows of light cut through it. Two of the men at the front of the procession waded into the water rather than follow the shallow length of the spit, which led like a gangplank almost as far as the boat. Once they were far enough away from the spit for the water to be up to their waists, they plunged forward and swam the long way round, heading out beyond the spit and then curving round to meet up with the boat on the other side.

Manfred increased his pace, realising that if everyone did that, they would reach the boat much more quickly than him. But he slowed down again once he realised that the fat waddling men in front of him, with check shirts and necks so burned they appeared to have been rubbing a rash, were not going anywhere. They walked slowly and evenly along the sand, their voluminous bottoms wobbling inside their shorts. One of them pushed his glasses back on his nose and looked round at the scenery. No one, it seemed, was in any particular rush to get home.

Manfred reached the end of the spit and started the slow shallow wade towards the boat. His mouth opened as he watched the boat sail some distance away; but then realised it was just bobbing along in the tide, because a while later it started bobbing back again. He could make out figures on the boat now; fat women, standing anxiously at the windows like mothers waiting for children to come home.

Manfred watched his feet trailing along in the shallow water; it was vaguely, sleepily pleasant. His toes were big and flat and the water trickled blue and yellow veins across his feet. The sand was soft and sensuous, moulded itself to his feet and made him want to close his eyes and lie down and let the water ripple around him. He made himself keep his eyes open and speeded up; the other men had put some distance between them again and he was trailing far behind. He blinked in the strong sunlight and wondered if it was a dream.

The first of the men swam up to the ladder on the side of the boat and climbed it, their muscles standing out in their arms as they heaved themselves over the top and into the welcoming arms of their wives, where each received his own hero's welcome. Manfred was in the water as far as his shins. He could see from the ladder that the boat was not out of his depth but he knew it would take a lot longer to wade than to swim. Well, they would just have to wait for him. The older, portlier men rolled their shorts up and walked comically with their arms hooked at the elbows to keep out of the water, their large bellies rolling about and slapping against the surface like beachballs.

Manfred was way behind now and experiencing another glimmer of nervousness. He walked more quickly but the sand would not let him make any greater speed. Ahead of him the overweight men were reaching the point where they too were giving up and plunging forward and trying to swim, their bald red heads moving up and down in the water like buoys.

The women cheered and clapped each time a man appeared over the side of the boat. When most of them were aboard Kem thanked them for their help. One or two of them looked expectantly at him, as if he might offer them a free beer, but he didn't.

Emily looked over the side of the boat and concentrated anxiously on Manfred. He was a small dark blob up to its knees in water, occasionally tripping forward and just righting himself in time before he fell over. He did not seem to move any closer forward, no matter how much she willed him too; and he was way behind the last of the fat men in their fifties. Why doesn't he just swim across, she wondered.

Kem watched the fat men flinging themselves inside like accidentally caught bloaters. They were patted and poked about like prize specimens, photographed and celebrated instead of being tossed back into the water. Concerned that the extra weight would ground the boat again, Kem ordered Ali to move the boat another thirty feet or so into the bay.

Manfred was tantalisingly close to the boat but it kept shifting away from him as quickly as he seemed to gain ground on it. He had to lunge forward more each time to stay the same distance away from the boat. Each time he did so he got a larger mouthful of water.

He could see Emily above him, looking down serenely, as still and calm as a statue. He tried to keep her image in his mind and to concentrate on it, as if it would help him reach the boat and save him from drowning. It was useful to have an icon or talisman to hold onto; as long as she was there, Manfred refused to believe he would drown. Kem knows what he's talking about, he told himself. He would not send us off to do this if he thought there was any danger. And Emily said everything would be okay.

Manfred was up to his waist. Each large step he took descended so far into the soft sand that he did not get any purchase to move further forward. He tried to take smaller steps, but this meant he travelled very slowly and used up lots of energy. The shorter men were out of their depth now and swimming quickly towards the boat. Manfred, being tall, was still able to wade slowly.

Glancing up occasionally Manfred realised he had misjudged the height of the ladder on the boat. He still reckoned it was within his depth, but it would be up to his neck; he would have to leap up to the boat when he reached it. He ignored a surge of panic but the process of ignoring it made his legs weak and he stumbled forward. Waves created by the boat reached him and made it even harder to stay above water.

Up to his neck now, he frequently tripped, his face pushing into the water. Only by trying to stay calm did his body bob to the surface and enable him to feel confident to continue walking.

The sand fell away; the ground banked suddenly and he could see a darker patch of sea in front of him. He tried to grip the ground with his feet but his toes skimmed the sand. There was nothing underneath him and he felt himself floating; the muscles in his legs were tired and each limb felt independent of the others. He turned round and flailed in the direction from which he had come, but his body was heavy in the water and refused to move. He trod water but the flow of the tide carried him sideways and he gasped and opened his mouth to suck in as much air as he could, anticipating going under.

Travelling powerlessly in the force of the tide, one of Manfred's feet skimmed past some sand and after a moment both feet made brief contact. He dug his toes in and thankfully, joyfully felt himself walking again. He could just keep his head above water and tried to make himself breathe calmly and not panic. The sand slipped away again, his legs sprang up behind him and his face went underwater. He floated for a while then sank beneath the surface.

He vaguely managed a kind of doggy-paddle, which was more a wired-in response than a conscious attempt to swim. He slipped under the water and struggled to the surface. He was tired and cold. It would be easier to give up and slip under the water; he could relax and it would be more comfortable to do what the water wanted to do. He looked around and realised that he had moved around so much that he was going in completely the wrong direction; he was so disoriented that he was now even further away from the boat than before.

Whereas before he had been panicking then telling himself it would be okay, now a cold logical fear came over him that insistently told him it would not be. He heard Emily's voice in his head, saying everything would be all right, and concentrated on this. But as the ground slowly, inexorably disappeared, he found himself thinking: what difference does it make whether Emily says everything is okay? Kem doesn't know it's going to be okay. You cling on to comments from people and they reassure you; but they have nothing to do with reality. He was facing reality now, which was that he was going to drown; and Emily saying everything would be okay had no power.

The other women on the boat sat eating bananas or drinking bottles of water, bored. Emily sat nervously on the edge of her seat. As Manfred neared the boat she lost sight of him and she told herself he would be all right. Manfred's ears were thick with water and he choked as water ran through the back of his nose and into his throat. The last couple of fat men reached the boat and heaved themselves up onto the steps. Manfred's head went underneath the water each time he lunged forward.

The water surged and foamed as the boat moved further into the bay. Down by the ladder, Manfred was invisible to Emily. He did not realise the boat was moving. Stumbling forward and treading water, he thought he was simply unable to reach it. Waves met over his head. Unused to being immersed in water the loudness of it confused him and his eyes stung. The feeling of water filling his ears and nose made him claustrophobic. Concentrating on holding his breath and breathing when he was safely above water distracted him from concentrating on reaching the ladder. The boat moved further away. His limbs had no energy in them.

No one on the boat raised an alarm or even knew he was where he was; he imagined Emily appearing round the corner to rescue him but knew this would not going to happen. He looked up; he could not see whether she was there or not. He went under the water and saw a void.

I really love her, a voice inside his head said. Dark green rushing clouds foamed around him. All those things about her that bother me – they're little things, they don't matter. What have I been doubtful about, he thought, as a stream of bubbles from his mouth formed in slow motion and dissipated into the nothingness. She's a bit quiet, a bit fussy – his head emerged above the water and the roaring sound of the water and the smell of diesel from the back end of the boat almost overpowered him – these things were nothing. He wanted to spend his life with her. He wished he had realised this before, because then he could have told her.

I shouldn't have done this, he thought. I should have been more firm. He felt this with such clarity that it was as if someone else had said it to him. He disappeared under the water.

Emily stood up decisively and went to find Kem. He was in the poky cabin, whistling as he tried to untie knots in the rope. She tapped him urgently on the shoulder and he turned to see a distraught woman gabbling incoherently. He shrugged and turned away, hoping this would make her calm down and talk more slowly. But it seemed to irritate her more; she hammered her fists on his back until he turned and clamped both her thin, white wrists under one hand. He held her so firmly that the energy that was making her fists move made her body jump up and down behind a motionless arm.

He raised his eyebrows and waited until she calmed down. When she did so he let her go. She put her hands over her face then ran her fingers through her dishevelled hair and spoke more slowly. 'Manfred isn't back yet,' she said. 'I think he's in trouble.'

'Okay,' he said, shrugging as if to say that there was no need to get so upset. He walked past her and up the steps to the main part of the boat and she followed him. 'Do not worry,' he said, turning his head back to talk to her as he walked along swiftly and decisively. 'We turn the boat back and I jump in and rescue him.'

'Thank you,' said Emily.

'There is no problem. He will not come to harm. There is no problem.'

It was silent under the water as Manfred's legs lifted up beneath him. Like a cork he bobbed to the surface. To his surprise, he found himself floating on his back with his head above water, gasping for breath. His instinct was to move his legs down; when he did this, he went under the water again. The second time he bobbed to the surface, his lungs aching and stretching for air, he remembered not to lower his legs but to allow them to go where the water wanted to take them. Moving nothing but his head, which he lifted slowly out from the water, he found he was float-ing; rolling slightly, but floating.

He stretched his legs and arms out and floated comfortably. For a few moments he lay there, breathing slowly until his heart stopped hammering in his chest. Looking around, he saw the boat bobbing about behind him.

He turned over in the water and found himself swimming. It was easy. You kick your legs in the water and you move towards the boat. He did not move fast, but he was only ten feet or so from the boat and by stretching his fingers to their extremities he could almost reach it. His legs dropped underneath him again after he had touched the boat but before he could get hold of it. He made several lunges, propelling himself as if he were a flying fish in order to strike the side of the boat. He held on to a ridge, his knuckles white, and breathed heavily. His fear disappeared as he held on to the solid hull of the boat; he closed his eyes and held his head against the wood. The boat smelt of pine and warmth and the sea.

When he had his breath back he shunted sideways along the

boat, the movement reminding him of clinging on to the side of the swimming pool during abandoned lessons at school. He worked his way along until he reached the steps, crawled up the ladder more with his arms than his legs and tipped over the side. The last thing he saw before he passed out were lots of large German bosoms crowding over his head, like clouds coming together before rain.

The women hauled Manfred into the boat just as Kem appeared with Emily behind him. 'There you are,' Kem said, relieved. Emily pushed past him and made her way into the mass of bodies and sarongs. The women clucked and made a channel for her through their sea of flesh; she put Manfred's head in her lap and wiped his face and hair with her sarong. He came round, choking and struggling. When he looked up his eyes were glassy and staring. Emily clutched him tightly until he coughed because he could not breathe. His hair was flattened to his skull like seaweed clinging to a rock. For a few moments he concentrated on breathing, then when he tried to say something to her, found that he couldn't.

They sat alongside the rail. They looked at the serene mountainside and then the beach, like a penny seen from its side, slowly sinking behind them until it disappeared. Everything seemed calm and quiet and harmless. Kem, passing through the boat on a beer selling trip, put a hand on Manfred's shoulder.

'You okay?' he asked, gruffly but benignly. Manfred nodded and trembled, afraid he was going to cry. He was cold and his lips tasted of salt. He bit his tongue until it stung. Kem patted Manfred briskly on the arm and went away, satisfied. Emily ignored him when he went. Manfred put his head against Emily's shoulder so that she would not see the tears pricking his eyes.

She hugged him close to her and he shivered.

She wanted to tell him how concerned she had been, but felt unable to. She opened her mouth to say that she had gone to get help, to reassure him that she had been thinking about him, but decided against it. He would be embarrassed by this and would prefer her not to make a fuss. Let him calm down before she said anything; let him speak first. She rubbed his arms and chest and back, trying not only to rub warmth into him but also to impart the communication that she had tried to do something about it. She knew that he had known that in the end, everything would be okay.

Manfred, in as much as his thoughts were coherent as he looked blankly out of the window, felt a failure. He could not swim, he had said he could not swim and no one had taken any notice of him. Kem had sent him off reassuring him that he would not have to swim. He had gone out of his depth to reach the boat and only got there by the discovery that when you have to swim, you find you can swim.

'I'm useless,' he murmured, so quietly that she did not hear him. He dozed against her shoulder, waking a minute or so later thinking it had been half an hour.

He was drenched; neither of them had brought a towel. Although it was still warm in the boat, the sun was not strong enough to dry out thick, wet cotton. Manfred, deciding he need-ed to do something about how much he was shivering, stood up and took his shorts off. He hung them over the edge of the boat. This attracted one or two glances from the German women who were sitting on the other side, but by now Manfred did not care.

His pants were soaking wet as well; they clung to him and he tried to pull them away from his body. When the shorts were dry he would go into the bathroom and change the pants for the shorts. Feeling the shorts from time to time, he realised it would take a long time.

Manfred fidgeted and watched the German women, who were talking quietly. Compared to how loud and exuberant they were earlier on, they were subdued and quiet. Several of the women were slumped against the wooden struts of the boat, as if they wanted to lie down and go to sleep. Emily nodded towards them. 'If they're down here,' she said, 'that must mean some of the sun loungers are free upstairs. Why don't you lie up there for a little while; it'll help you dry out.' She gave him her bag, which had sun cream and sunglasses in it.

Manfred nodded and padded up the staircase to the top deck. On his way up, he bought a bottle of beer from Ali. When he had gone Emily rearranged the shorts on the rail of the boat and tied the cords to a nail that was sticking out of the wood, to prevent the shorts blowing away. They would not have been there when he came back if she had not secured them; she felt pleased to be useful to him without him knowing.

Manfred emerged on the top deck and breathed deeply. Emily was right; the sun was much warmer up here. Two tanned, muscular men nudged each other when they saw Manfred in his pants and carrying Emily's bag. They had wide, confident smiles, with mouths full of perfect teeth. Manfred met their gaze and then sat cautiously on the only available seat. He opened his bottle of beer, drank a few mouthfuls and set the bottle by his side.

The lounger wobbled slightly on the surface of the boat; it was not attached properly, or was not put up fully. It wobbled, but he ignored it. He tried to sit normally. It wobbled, and he lifted his arms and tensed his legs to compensate. Lying back, he opened his legs and felt the warmth of the sun working on his cold, wet pants. The lounger wobbled alarmingly. He felt his calves instinctively contract, then made them relax. He tried to ignore the German men and the way they lay proudly with their legs open and their Speedos bulging insolently.

Kem watched Manfred disappear and then approached Emily. She had gone back to her guidebook and looked up when he sat down next to her. For the second time that day, he took his sunglasses off.

'You had a good trip?' he asked, looking out to the headland.

'Yes, thank you, it was lovely,' murmured Emily.

Kem nodded and his mouth opened and showed his blunt, squat teeth as he narrowed his eyes.

'And Manfred,' he said casually, 'he had a good day?'

'Oh yes, I think so.'

'He was brave I think,' said Kem, 'having to reach the boat when he cannot swim.'

Emily put her book down on the bench beside her. 'He can't swim?' she said incredulously.

Kem looked at her with alarm. 'Er – no,' he said. 'You did not know?' He looked uncomfortable.

Emily stared at him. She could see a series of thoughts running across his eyes. He had been intending to placate any possible anger from Emily; he did not want his passengers to mutiny and demand their money back. Some English tourists had done this when the boat got grounded a couple of years previously, and he had had to stall and make up promises for the whole journey back. He wanted to avoid that for as long as possible; there was still a long journey ahead of them. He knew Emily would be docile, but wanted to find out from her what Manfred might be thinking. The news that Emily had not known that Manfred could not swim came as a worrying surprise. It might make the placid English girl rear up and go red and become unreasonable. He thought quickly.

'But,' he said, 'I knew that he was never in any real danger. I would have turned the boat back for him, if he was.'

'Yes,' said Emily frostily, 'yes, you would have done, wouldn't you?'

Kem beamed. 'I am glad you understand,' he said convivially, rubbing her shoulder. She remembered the way the men had pawed her on the way out and she recoiled.

'Well,' he said, slapping his knees firmly and then standing up, 'I must be getting back to Ali, to check he is steering the boat safely and properly.'

'Good idea,' said Emily bluntly. When Kem had gone she read and re-read the paragraph in her book.

The sea became rougher. The gulet was approaching a headland; there were white patches ahead where two tides met. Manfred felt queasy. The sun was still hot but there was a strong wind which brought the smell of diesel up from the engines. The lounger wobbled about beneath him; he clung on and felt a spasm in his stomach. He leant over the side to be sick, but nothing happened. The movement caused the lounger to imbalance and it tipped over beneath him. The muscular men roared with laughter, their sunglasses making their eyes seem alien and evil, like flies' eyes.

Manfred stood but the swaying of the boat made him lose his grip and he slipped against the side of the boat. The wooden rim made a cracking sound as it impacted on his ribs, and Manfred vomited over the side of the boat. The vomit caught in the wind and sprayed like confetti over some sea birds which were gaining and losing height as they battled against the conflicting winds. The German men fell about laughing, wrapping their arms against their sides and shaking their heads. The bottle rolled around at Manfred's feet, fizzing and spilling beer over his feet and shins.

The sun beat fiercely down. Manfred made his way slowly downstairs, knocking his elbows and hips against the sides of the narrow staircase as the boat rolled. He still felt sick and, as he realised as soon as he was in the shade, he was burning from the sun. Emily was chatting to another new friend, showing him something in her guidebook and finding out what he thought about it. When she saw Manfred, she dropped the book and led him to the table. She staggered as she did so, not realising how choppy the water had become before she tried to walk.

He leant against the side of the boat, curling his feet up under him. Emily sat beside him and rubbed his back. 'Where's my bag?' she asked.

'I've left it upstairs,' he said, struggling to his feet.

'It's okay,' she said, pushing him back down again, 'I'll go.'

'No, it's all right,' he said. As they tried to stop each other having to go, stumbling against each other as the boat heaved, their path was blocked by one of the Germen men. He swung down the ladder, his muscles bulging, apparently unaffected by the motion of the boat. Manfred looked at him nervously.

'Is this your bag?' he said in careful, immaculate English. Emily nodded. 'Thank you,' she said, blushing.

The man took his glasses off and nodded at Manfred. Then, as if he could not think of anything else to say, he went back upstairs.

Manfred looked outside at the choppy water and puffed his cheeks out, as if this would stop him vomiting again. He watched the sea churn up and down and imagined the beer churning up and down in his otherwise empty stomach. He leant over the side of the boat and for the fourth or fifth time, made the motions of vomiting, but nothing happened. He sat back tired with the exertion his stomach was forcing him to make.

All he wanted to do was lie down in a quiet, dark room. He could not relax; the motion of the boat meant he was constantly using muscles he didn't know he had in order to stay balanced. Lying down on the benches was not an option; he had to compensate continually for the motion of the boat, and so his body was tense, not relaxed, and he certainly wouldn't be able to doze.

He lay on the floor, but Emily made him get up because she said it was dirty. The rougher weather had made the air a few degrees colder; Emily rummaged around in her bag and found a T-shirt and put it on over her bikini top. As he rested against her shoulder, the distinctive, light smell of her washing powder was a reassuring sensation. It reminded him of home and was a beacon of familiarity in the alien, unknown world he was in.

This struck him as interesting, despite his tiredness; he had never consciously noticed the smell of her washing powder before, but now it was the most important thing in the world to him. He pushed his nose fully against her shoulder and breathed in deeply, breathing out through his nose, and stayed like that for several minutes, closing his eyes and not wanting to move, until she started to ache and made him shift position. Feeling a little better, he sat up and looked around.

Manfred listened to the ever-present creaking of the wood. It was clearly an old boat; he wondered if they ever checked it was seaworthy. He remembered the wrecked boat outside the village by the beach, and an uncomfortable feeling prickled the back of his neck. Emily untied the shorts from the rail. 'They're almost dry,' she said, handing them to him. 'How are your pants?'

'Getting better,' he murmured. He glanced across at the German women, who watched him intently to see what he would do next. Emily, on a sudden resolve, got up to find Kem and get some answers out of him. She wanted to emphasise to him that Manfred had been in danger and to tell him he should have been looking out for him, since he had known he couldn't swim.

'Don't go away,' said Manfred, not looking up at her but speaking urgently. Emily sat down and hugged him.

V

The boat passed the headland and the swaying lessened. One of the two German women came over and babbled away incomprehensibly to Manfred. She spoke no English, but her face was full of consternation and she knitted her hands together limply in sympathy. Manfred tried to appear receptive and encouraging, despite his tiredness. The woman waved a towel at him, muttered another volley of German, and thrust the towel in his hand.

He went to the bathroom and took his pants off. He felt uncomfortable about drying his genitals with the woman's towel, but was still so damp, and the towel was so fluffy and warm, that he shrugged and enjoyed it.

He pulled on the shorts and felt warm and comfortable. He sat down on the toilet, closing his eyes with the bliss of feeling normal. There was the familiar smell of acrid, stale faeces which never disappears from toilets on boats. The smell brought to mind a sailing holiday he had gone on five or six years previously and had mostly forgotten about. Six people in a 30 foot yacht; it was when Manfred had started to lose some of his inbuilt caution and sense of privacy, and had started sleeping naked. He had the same doubts then as now about going on a boat, but had felt unable to admit to his friends that he could not swim.

He remembered rounding Start Point in Devon and the boat riding twenty or thirty foot waves, and everyone clinging on for dear life and screaming and laughing as the cold waves hit them in the face. They were all dressed in brightly coloured yellow and red anoraks, zipped up above their heads, and thus resembled blobby dabs of paint in a colourless, violent seascape, like a painting by Turner. He remembered seeing everything through a permanent mist that steamed in his glasses, and through drops of water on the lenses, which he could not wipe because he could not let go of the chrome railing of the boat.

Manfred shook his head as he watched a beetle run up the

pine door of the gloomy, cramped bathroom. The memory of the bitter chill of the English Channel made him feel cold, and he shivered. Now, with his eyes open, he felt hot again. A vertical streak of yellow light ran along the side of the ill-fitting door. The beetle ran into this light, its brown back illuminated momentarily before it disappeared.

Sitting in a dark toilet on a gulet, details of the forgotten holiday like the metal rail of the boat and the brown, patterned, uncomfortable cushioned bunks which smelled of tobacco, came back to him with sudden clarity. The slicing wind which ripped through the thick, insulated anoraks; the stale, airless smell each morning after the windows had been closed all night; the aching tiredness that he experienced when they had to get up at 6am to catch the tide; the yellow sunrises and the crisp, clear air; the vigorous concentration of getting paralysingly drunk each evening and the surprising appetite he had for this after being cooped up in the boat all day.

He wondered how he had forgotten all these details and why they were coming back so vividly now. Each memory followed quickly on the last and they were all triggered by the particular smell of the toilet – the heads, he remembered they were called – which was integral to the holiday, but which he had not smelled anywhere since.

He wondered why he had not been scared when they had rounded Start Point and the boat had tipped and yawed. At times, they had been alarmingly high up in the air, fearfully glancing down at the green, icy water as if on a rollercoaster, then dropping like a plane losing height, leaving their stomachs suspended somewhere above them.

He would have been scared had it not been for a conversation he had had that morning with the captain, who had warned him what the day held. He drew on a piece of paper what the yacht looked like without water. Protruding from the bottom of the boat was a long, spearheaded fin, which reached as far below the water line as the mast was above it. So although it may appear that the boat is being flung about on the surface and could easily capsize, the captain told him, it is actually firmly rooted in the water.

This was all that Manfred had needed to feel confident that they would be safe. Belief, Manfred thought as he listened to the gentle trickling of water in the pipes and shifted his bottom on the seat, is all about being given a piece of information, or having someone telling you that everything will be all right, and sticking to that shred of information, however thin or unlikely it might be. It's about having faith in the person who tells you it will be all right; and the strength of that faith is based on how confident they sound It's when you have no shred of information, or no faith in the person who talks to you, that you become afraid of life.

'No,' the captain had said in his gravelly, authoritative voice. 'You do not need to worry about the yacht capsizing. It – will – not.' He thumped his fist on the chart table on each word and observed Manfred with pale blue seaworthy eyes, years of experience and knowledge emanating from him. He made Manfred believe and trust him more effectively than any hypnotism by saying this. Had they not had that brief conversation, Manfred would have been petrified. The boat plummeted; at one point the spray forced Manfred across the deck of the boat and he ended up sprawled across the wet floor by the opposite railing. The others quickly righted him and he held on to the other railing before the rollercoaster leaped and dived again a moment later; but Manfred was not scared. He had faith.

He shook his head thinking about it now. There was a banging on the door and Manfred jumped up and opened the door. 'Sorry,' he said wanly to the uncomfortable looking man waiting outside. He squinted in the bright sunlight; he had got used to the cool sauna feel of the dark bathroom.

'No,' he remembered the captain saying, 'the only dangerous

thing is if you ground the boat; that's when you risk the bottom ripping out of it. Then you really are in trouble.' He had scratched his beard and stared into space, remembering. 'I was in a boat once and we grounded. Tore away from the bank and got going again, thought nothing of it. Just as we were entering port it started to sink. Five minutes earlier and we'd all have drowned. As it was it was touch and go.'

Manfred walked back to Emily feeling the lightness in his legs and a pulsating in his neck that made him wonder if he was going to be sick again.

Emily asked Kem if there was any food they could buy. He told them that unfortunately there wasn't. 'But you can have beer, ginger beer, apple tea, coffee.' It was now nearly five o'clock and they both felt weak and hungry; it had been hours since their slim lunch. Thinking of the chicken again made him feel queasy. Manfred looked across at the posh woman and wondered if she had a secret supply of cucumber sandwiches in her canvas bag. His mouth watered at the idea, which appeared in front of his mind with great clarity and included the aroma and the taste.

Manfred closed his eyes and rested his head on Emily's arm. When he opened his eyes the boat was in the open sea again and they were swaying up and down rhythmically. He still felt unwell, but at least his stomach had settled and the smell of diesel had lessened. He looked around, trying not to imagine what would happen if the bottom of the boat suddenly fell out. It might travel a hundred miles, or fifty, or ten, and the movement of the hull would be slowly worrying whatever damage there was, and eventually it would split apart.

He looked around the cabin. There were two or three lifebelts slung casually along the shelves that lined the ceiling. He would make sure he grabbed one for himself and one for Emily at the first sign of anything happening. He had had one brush with fate that day and no one had seemed bothered; he would not feel guilty or selfish if he grabbed the only available lifebelts and everyone else had to take their chances. It had been survival of the fittest so far. No one had looked out for him when he had been in trouble. He nodded decisively. He had to be blunt with himself or he would dither in the event of anything happening.

But the boat is sturdily made, he told himself. Nothing will happen. He listened to the steady, rhythmic creaking of the wood. He looked at Emily; she was smiling slightly, imagining being home. She was too tired to keep her eyes open, but it was impossible to sleep. Manfred did not express his fears about the boat. What would be the point; she could do nothing about it if anything happened. If he told her, she would just worry. Better to let her be content and not know about it. He felt as if he was betraying her by not telling her; he bit his lip. But it was the right thing to do to stay quiet; wasn't it? He wished he could ask someone.

He looked out of the window to see if they were nearly home; he tried to restrict these hopeful glances now, as if the longer he avoided each look, the more quickly they would get there. The land moved painfully slowly. It was easy to believe that they would never arrive, no matter how long they travelled for. There were at least two or three more bays to come before they approached their village; forty-five minutes at least, he estimated, an hour probably, and another fifteen minutes beyond that before they would be walking on dry land. He concentrated on the image of being on land, willing it to become true. The concept of being on an unmoving, quiet surface now seemed impossible.

He promised himself that he would remember what it was like on this boat at future times when he was bored and discontented. He would remember the agony of being here, and appreciate the joy of being on dry land and being able to relax and not move, and be dry and comfortable. Ordinary life would never be boring again; it would be pleasurable.

He knew that within a day of being back on land, he would have forgotten this promise to himself. They were both exhausted, incapable of saying anything to each other and just wanting to be home. They lay across each other on the bench, but it was difficult to relax even when doing this. Everything took forever. The scenery paled to monotony. It was definitely taking longer to get back than it had to come out; they had been travelling more than four hours on the return journey, and were still not in sight of home. They were sailing against the tide, Manfred supposed.

The gangly photographer made his way round the boat and showed the passengers their pictures. Manfred wondered where he had disappeared to, how he had got them developed spo quickly, and when he had got back on to the boat. Emily told him she thought he rejoined them when they met up with the large boat again, after the time spent on the beach.

Most people bought the pictures out of politeness. The photographer handed Emily the photos and she sat up, yawning and blinking at them. The first showed Emily, part of her face in shadow, with an attractive chunk of mountain and sea behind her. The photo of Manfred was taken square-on and showed him glaring up at the camera.

'How much are they?' Emily asked, and the camera man smiled, tipping his head from side to side. 'They are very cheap,' he said.

'Yes,' said Emily, 'but how much?' She had learnt how to get straight answers by being direct; it had taken a while, as it was so out of character for her. But the price the photographer quoted was very modest, and Emily nodded and reached into her purse.

'Don't buy the one of me,' said Manfred. Emily looked at it, and nodded. 'No, okay,' she agreed. Yesterday, she thought, him saying this would probably have upset her; she would have wanted the photo. There was also one of them together, which Manfred refused to buy. The photographer looked upset at his brusqueness.

Manfred decided he would be happier when he had eaten something. At least Emily had not kicked up a fuss about the photographs; he had expected her to insist on buying them. He squeezed her hand and she rested her head against him. He felt a prickle of excitement tensing his penis; perhaps he was feeling better. The boat had not sunk. Everything was all right.

The sky was yellower and the sun began its long, slow preparations for setting. Manfred bought another beer from Kem in a last-ditch attempt at alleviating his torpor. It almost worked. He had had five or six beers during the course of the day and he wished they had had a little more effect. Kem was still chatty, asking Manfred random questions to test his English and smiling encouragingly when Manfred couldn't be bothered to reply.

'Very yellow sunsets, aren't they?' Manfred said.

'Yes.'

'Not like in the morning, where you get lots of purples and reds. That's what I thought the sunsets would be like.'

Kem shrugged. 'Sometimes we do, sometimes we don't.' He got up and walked round the boat one more time, trying to sell the last few bottles of beer.

'Look,' said Manfred on an intake of breath, 'that's our bay ahead.' He squeezed Emily's arm.

'Is it really?' she asked, finding it difficult to focus. Manfred nodded.

'How can you tell?'

'The boat's heading towards the bay,' he said, 'as opposed to heading to the edge of the land.' Throughout the trip Ali had navigated by the ancient method of aiming for the furthest point of land that jutted out, steering away from it as they approached it, then as the next bay opened up ahead, aiming for the next visible extremity of land. Now, the boat was heading into harbour. It was nearly seven o'clock. The sun nudged the jagged shadow of the mountain and the temperature dropped several degrees in a few seconds. Manfred and Emily looked at each other, stunned at how quickly it became cold. They sat closer together. Emily put her hands under Manfred's T-shirt and Manfred put his hands under his legs.

A violent shudder racked the boat. Manfred gripped the seat. His body tensed up and he got ready to run for the life jackets. Preparing for sudden movement, his bowels slackened. The calm, weary faces of everyone around him appeared surreal in Manfred's heightened state of tension; no one else seemed fussed while he was clenching and unclenching his hands.

But nothing happened. The creaking gradually disappeared and the boat fell into silence and continued its steady journey. As the minutes passed, Manfred felt safe again. The journey ended without incident.

The posh woman stumbled as she walked down the bouncy gangplank to the shore. 'Well,' she said, disentangling her broken heel from a splintering gap in the wood, 'that's just the final straw.' She tottered away, her husband following her silently. Manfred could not remember him having said a word all day.

Emily and Manfred were the last off the boat. Kem stood by the entrance like an air hostess at the door of a plane, thanking everyone as they went and asking, once again, if they had had a good time.

Manfred looked at him and said nothing. 'You have a good time?' Kem asked. Emily nodded. 'Well,' she said timidly, 'perhaps if it had been advertised as a swimming and sunbathing trip, we wouldn't have come.'

'Ah well,' said Kem. The sun had gone but Kem did not remove his glasses. He helped Emily and Manfred along the plank and onto land. Manfred looked at Emily but her eyes and body language did not reveal what she was thinking. As he could not catch her eye, he stopped looking at her and squeezed her hand as they walked along.

It was not as cold on land as it had been in the last half hour at sea. They looked back briefly. Kem was chatting volubly to Ali, waving his hands expressively. Ali, half-listening, wound the guy ropes round the bollards on the jetty. The sun disappeared behind the mountain on the edge of the bay. The orange sky turned a dull, metallic blue.

VI

'You choose the restaurant,' Manfred said. 'Whichever one you fancy.'

She shook her head. 'Let's just go to the first one we see. I'm sure it'll be lovely.'

The waiter welcomed them in and sat them by a long white-washed wall. 'You have been on a boat?' he asked as they settled in the chairs, which scraped against the uneven floor.

'Yes,' said Manfred. 'We've been on a boat.'

'You like drinks?'

'Oh yes, we like drinks.' He ordered a ten year old bottle of wine.

'Are you sure?' said Emily, leaning forward so that the waiter would not hear. 'Don't go mad.'

'I'm celebrating our survival,' he said. Yesterday her caution would have annoyed him. It didn't seem to matter any more. The things that bothered him about her were unimportant. He still hadn't told her how worried he had been about the bottom of the boat ripping away. Perhaps he would later.

The wine, which was delicious, cost about the same as a bottle of house wine at home, so it was not really 'going mad'. Also, he thought, as the waiter poured the wine and Emily tasted it and said it was lovely, he should go down to Kem's shop tomorrow and complain and tell him to get his boat checked and demand his money back. Perhaps he would.

'What was that food you had the other night?' Emily asked. 'All those bits and pieces?'

'Meze.'

'I'll have that then.' She patted the table decisively with both hands. He watched her closely when the food arrived, and she ate placidly. More doubts disappeared. He found her company entrancing and magical. The wine vanished and he ordered another bottle. The waiter beamed and trotted away.

Manfred realised he loved her, and could never do without her. He wondered what she was thinking.

A child, evidently the son of the proprietor, played with a wooden car on the outside step. Occasionally he looked up as someone walked past.

Emily watched the child as he ran his car up and down against the kerb. The car picked up a cloud of dust under its wheels. Emily bit her lip and tried not to think about him too much. She knew she had made the right decision and was content. If Manfred didn't want children she was prepared to accept the fact.

Manfred sipped his wine and looked at the boy. He would tense up as he heard footsteps, then lose interest when the passers-by walked on. Evidently he was primed to run in and get his dad if they stopped to look at the menu. Manfred put his wine glass down and toyed with it, stirring it so that the liquid inside developed a pattern like a propeller rotating.

He remembered Emily saying something about children the

other night. He did not want to talk about children because he did not want her to think he was pressuring her, or using the magic of the honeymoon to make her say yes if she didn't really want to say yes. He would talk to her about it when they got home, he decided. When they were themselves again, he reasoned, instead of the honeymoon couple.

He would like a boy, he decided. Or a girl. He didn't really mind. No – definitely a girl.

Or a boy. He would have to think about it. He went back to his food. Emily watched him and resisted the temptation to run round the side of the table and hug him. Looking round, she thought, why do I have to resist the temptation? She was on honeymoon. She ran round the side of the table and hugged him. He looked up in surprise and she kissed him. By the entrance, the boy jumped up as a couple stood arm in arm, looking at the menu. He rushed to the back to find his father. The toy car lay on its side in the dust, its wheels spinning.

Emily wanted to tell Manfred that she loved him. She made circles on the tablecloth with her finger and bit her lip, and opened her mouth, then closed it again. It was not the right time. She knotted her fingers together anxiously. She did not want him to think that she hadn't cared about what had happened on the boat, or hadn't noticed, or hadn't done anything about it, or hadn't realised how brave he had been. He could think any of these things.

But he seemed happy at the moment and she wanted them to enjoy the meal together; she didn't want to remind him because he might get upset. Or he might get cross, and start complaining about Kem. Later she would tell him she loved him.

She tried to imagine how she would feel if things had happened differently this afternoon. She tried, but found that she couldn't. Her mind was unable to conceive of it. Her brain refused to let her go down that path, which she was pleased about, because it would have driven her beyond horror and terror.

Manfred wondered why she remained silent about the events on the boat. He wanted to talk about it, but surely if she wanted to she would say something. He took this to mean that she did not want to talk about it, so he stayed silent. Reflecting on the trip, he realised that what he had feared most was not dying, because dying was nothing; it was impossible to be scared of nothing. What he had feared was losing Emily. It was as if she had been about to die, not him, because if he died, it would be Emily who would disappear from his life.

What had made him unhappiest of all was the idea of not having the rest of his days with her – all the times they had in front of them, the experiences, the days out, the ordinary life, the rows, the bad times. All this was due to them, and was essential, and explained why he experienced the frustration and the fury of being about to die. What was right would have been denied him. It was right that they were sitting here now; it was right and good.

He sipped his wine and looked at her. They listened to the crickets and the gentle buzzing of mosquitoes. They heard music faintly travelling across the street from a nearby house. The music faded in and out of audibility as the breeze carried it over to them or took it away. They said nothing to each other. Manfred closed his eyes, and a smile formed on Emily's mouth.

The waiter came out and asked them if everything was okay; he seemed concerned, as if worried that they were unhappy because they weren't talking to each other, or that their silence meant there was something wrong with the food. Both murmured that everything was fine and that the food was wonderful. The waiter hurried away, full of anxiety. He came back with two free drinks.

They listened to the gentle murmurings of the waiter and his wife chatting in the kitchen, and the lazy sound of wide china dishes being placed on wooden tables. Manfred looked at Emily and her eyes sparkled. She drank her wine and glowed.

Manfred paid the bill before the waiter could see the sterling notes in his wallet. Now that they were used to the brown and red paper notes, the shiny English ones with their hologram and silver strip of sewn metal seemed exotic; a reversal of how it had been when they arrived. He left a generous tip. The waiter clapped his hands and brought them two glasses of a dark, muddy spirit that they could not identify, and begged them to return tomorrow night.

Walking along the narrow track to the hotel, listening to their feet scuffing the dirt, they looked at the boxes of over-ripe melons lying at the side of the road. A skinny dog rooted around in the dust, nosing tin cans.

'Why didn't you tell me you couldn't swim?' she asked eventually, tugging his arm.

He did not answer, but hugged her closer to him. The sound of grit scuffing under their feet suddenly seemed louder; almost as if it would drown out anything he said. Why hadn't he told her? He supposed it was because he was embarrassed, or because it had not occurred to him that it would be an issue until it was too late. In reality he did not why he did not or could not tell her. He still felt unable to say anything.

When he smiled at her and stayed silent, she did not think he was being moody.

They left their clothes in the hallway. He did not say he loved her as he had intended to, as they undressed and got into bed. Emily, still feeling the novelty of sleeping naked and vaguely believing that not wearing anything in bed was wrong, rolled around, enjoying the feeling of the sheets against her skin. Her pyjamas lay folded up on the table at the foot of the bed, where she had left them on the first day. She resolved that from now on she would always sleep naked. She nodded decisively, as if the nodding ensured it would happen.

She put her arm across him and rubbed the hairs on his chest. 'I love you,' she whispered, but his ear was flattened by her shoulder and he did not hear. Now that she thought about it, she could not recall him ever saying that he loved her.

She kissed him on the chest and shifted round. She moved her head up and down in the crook of his armpit, and the sensation reminded her of the boat. It seemed right not to make love. She hoped he did not mind, but she didn't have the energy to ask. He did not move as she lay there, so she knew he did not.

Manfred dreamt of foaming water and turtles. He swam, and the turtles swam around him. The water was viscous and emerald like green and white oil paint loosely mixed together.

One of the turtles swam up to him and used its flippers to propel him along in the water. 'Thank you,' said Manfred, turning round and smiling at the turtle.

'You're welcome,' said the turtle in a quiet, gentle voice.

Emily watched Manfred, who had fallen asleep before her as usual. She ran her hand through his hair. He was exhausted; there were deep lines under his eyes and his face looked mottled from being wet and uncomfortable all day. The tone of his skin seemed bleached; so much water had got into him that the colour had thinned. His eyes moved and she knew he was dreaming. She wondered what it was about, and where he was.

As she turned on her side towards him, she started to see images that did not make sense and hear snippets of imaginary conversations, and she knew that this meant she was about to fall asleep.

She clutched on to Manfred to prevent herself falling away from him. Her eyes closed of their own accord. There are two kinds of silence, she thought as she slipped into sleep – the kind of silence where you don't say anything, and the kind where you do.

In the morning, the sun was a huge, brilliant orange.

to drink at midsummer

I

The last hymn was *He who would Valiant Be*. Hugo sang boldly, loudly, confidently. Not always tunefully, but then three out of four isn't bad. Dena looked up at him from time to time as she watched him concentrate on the difficult notes. She often complimented him on the fact that he rarely missed them by more than a semitone. When the song ended, he sat down and felt the blood pumping round his system; that wonderful effect that singing in church never fails to produce.

The organ chords died away. There was the sudden noise of everyone sitting down, like dead leaves rustling. The wall by their pew glowed blue and red from the stained glass window on the opposite wall. Hugo experienced the familiar painful longing at the end of a church service for one more hymn. He felt his pulse beating in his fingers and put the hymnbook on the shelf in front of him. The red leather seemed to glow. He could still feel the book after he had let go of it. He had to resist the urge to bend its soft, smooth cover back and forth.

God was everywhere this morning. He was in the wood of the pews, inside Hugo's lungs as they tingled with the songs, and dancing about in the patterns of coloured light on the wall.

Everything seemed much brighter, clearer and more real when in church. It was the singing that did it. It made Hugo feel so rich, he was conscious of the existence of his body, his hands, his feet. He sighed and felt his throat and mouth and stomach breathing.

Hugo blundered out into the light and had the feeling of disorientation and dizziness, like when leaving a cinema. The human brain cannot cope with the cool darkness so suddenly being transformed into hot brightness. Hugo had to stand still and let his body adjust, feeling that if he did not do so he would fall over.

'Hello Hugo, having a vision?' The wry face of the vicar smiled at him. Hugo frowned. The vicar suffered from the curse of irony, like so many other people these days. Everything was ironic, according to some programme he had watched last week. Nothing was real or had any worth unless it could be expressed in ironic terms. What on earth did that mean? There was truth or there wasn't truth. Doesn't matter if you don't agree, or if you see the truth differently – but it's still one or the other.

At least, Hugo thought so. At least, Hugo knew what he meant and that was all that mattered. Presumably what the vicar found so amusing was that anyone these days should have such old-fashioned, serious belief. But wasn't that what the vicar was there for, to encourage the young to have faith? The vicar wasn't any younger than he was, but he made Hugo feel twenty years older. Everyone was cynical and negative nowadays.

Dena was close behind. She slipped her arm into Hugo's, said hello politely to the vicar and moved Hugo firmly towards the gate.

'You are funny, Hugo. Why did you stand there looking at him?'

'I felt a bit peculiar.'

'He made a little joke and you just stared at him.'

Hugo scratched his neck. Cars gleamed and reflected points

of bright sunlight as they moved away from the roadside. The congregation moved slowly along the road like a multicoloured stream of water.

They walked home and listened to the birds singing and the gentle clicking of their heels on the pavement. Hugo put his jacket on. It was a cool summer and, as Dena pointed out most days, it was difficult to believe it was August; there was not much warmth in the air. 'It'll be hot next week, apparently,' he said, continuing his thoughts out loud.

Dena looked at him; to her, his comment seemed apropos of nothing. 'Well yes,' she said, 'it's the summer, it jolly well should be.'

'Still nice though.' Hugo felt satisfied and calm and as he slipped his arm round his wife's waist he reflected contentedly that nothing could spoil this. They were safe together, safe in their pretty village, enclosed, protected, loved. 'I feel full of the joys of being alive today,' he said.

She nodded. 'Ooh, look,' she said, 'that shop's having a 50% sale.'

II

Hugo disappeared into the bedroom when Dena rang Yasmina. 'Yes, I know,' she said to Yasmina's echoey voice. 'I know. Oh, it can't be. Is it really? Well definitely next weekend then. Oh yes, we've got a map. We'll ring you if we can't find the house. Oh yes, I know, I'm sure we will. Oh, I know. I know. Bye then.'

Dena put the phone down and went into the bedroom. Hugo was sitting by the desk, intently reading *The Unbearable Lightness of Being* with a rapt expression on his face.

Dena stood in silence for a few moments. Hugo slowly

turned a page. Dena tried to make conversation. 'Is it as good as the film?'

Hugo looked up at her, a blank look on his face. He had taken the words in, but it took him a moment to put them together and work out what she had said. 'I don't know,' he replied eventually. 'I haven't seen the film.'

'Oh, it's really good.'

Hugo went back to the book.

'I've just talked to Yasmina.'

'Hmm.'

'We're going down next weekend.'

Hugo put the book down. '*Next* weekend?'

Dena looked at him with large round eyes. 'You didn't have anything else planned, did you?'

'Well, no, but...'

'If we don't just say, right, let's do it next weekend, we'll never go at all.' She waved a hand dismissively into the ether, as if indicating all the other lost weekends when they hadn't gone to visit Yasmina that had been profligately thrown away.

Hugo picked the book up again.

'She said we haven't seen her since this time last year.' Dena put her hands on her hips. 'I thought you were going to make the arrangements this time.'

'Really?' Why does she call it 'arrangements', thought Hugo; it's a phone call, not an international peace conference. He licked his finger and traced it alongside the words on the page, trying to concentrate on taking them in.

'Yes. Hugo, you could take a little more interest in our friends.'

'She's your friend.'

'No, she's our friend. She's one of the few people we became friends with together.'

'I don't see why that makes her any more important,' he murmured. 'It's not my fault you don't like any of my friends and I don't like yours.'

Dena pulled a face. 'Now that's not true. You do like my friends.'

No I don't, thought Hugo. 'Mmm,' he said.

'And it's not that I don't like yours.'

Yes it is, thought Hugo. 'I know,' he said.

'I just don't... understand them. I'm sure they're all very nice people, underneath.'

'Mmm...' Hugo's mouth formed the shapes of words as he read. He had got to a good bit.

'Well anyway, we're going to see her next weekend.' Dena started picking things up on the mantelpiece and repositioning them. She moved around Hugo rearranging flowers and plumping cushions. For the first two or three years of their marriage this had irritated Hugo when he was reading, but he was used to it now and it did not distract him any more. He reached the end of the chapter and looked up at Dena, who had moved on to the picture frames on the sideboard.

'How on earth are we supposed to find this new house of hers anyway?' he asked. He turned the page. He always liked getting to the end of a chapter; there was a sense of achievement in being able to turn over a blank page, a feeling of getting on in life.

'I've got a map.'

He shrugged.

'What's wrong with you Hugo, I thought you were full of the joys of being alive today.'

'I am. I just don't see the point of gallivanting off into the back of beyond to meet up with some drippy girl who spends half the day talking to herself.'

'It's Wiltshire, it's hardly the back of beyond. And she does-n't spend all day talking to herself,' she added.

Yes she does, thought Hugo. 'No, all right.' He went back to the book.

'Okay she talks to herself a lot,' Dena conceded, 'but no more than you do.'

Hugo looked up and after a long pause, smiled at her. Dena stood with her arms folded and a cross expression, and her face was red. Then she relaxed, walked over to him and hugged him.

'Come here, you,' she murmured. All was well with the world again. The cloud passed. Hugo beamed like the sun. Dena sat on his lap and put her arms round his neck.

Hugo glanced at the number of his page then dropped the book on the desk.

III

'Where on earth is Stonend anyway?' he complained, poring over the south west of England.

Dena pointed. 'It's there,' she said. 'Look, don't worry. I can direct us as far as Andover and we'll only have to look at the map from there.'

'And once we find Stonend, how will we find the actual house? You haven't got a street plan.'

'Stop grumbling. Yasmina says it's really easy.'

Hugo groaned. 'I've heard that before. Yasmina was the one who said that getting to Docklands was easy.'

'We only missed the first half of the show.'

So it came to pass that at 9.25 on Saturday morning a battered Volvo chugged down Cromwell Drive. Hugo and Dena tended not to pack as such, but just to put everything they needed for the weekend into the back of the car. Between courses of breakfast consisting of pieces of toast and olives eaten from the hand whilst wandering about the house, as they noticed each item that they thought they might want they picked it up and took it out to the car and threw it into the boot. By the time the car was full, they knew they probably had everything they would need.

It looked like they were going to a jumble sale as they drove towards the motorway with cardigans, tatty paperbacks, scruffy pullovers, clocks, underwear, razor blades, skirts and badly squeezed tubes of toothpaste piled up on the back seat. Reaching the M4, Hugo expected traffic but found none, and they made excellent time. 'It'll slow down once we get on the smaller roads,' commented Dena, munching on an apple she had found in the glove box.

But once into deepest Wiltshire the roads were long and straight, disappearing as in a technical diagram to a vanishing point that shimmered on the horizon. Vast fields of mustardy yellow lazed expansively on either side of them. The road was dusty and sulphurous clouds passed idly beside them from time to time, as they had nothing better to do. Hugo and Dena wound their windows down and dropped the sun guards, and rested their elbows on the windows. Dena felt her elbow slowly burning.

They chugged along at 55. Dena screwed her eyes up to look at a sloping field that had appeared in front of them. 'There's something odd about that hill,' she said. Hugo glanced across, unimpressed by the markings on the field.

'It's a crop circle!' cried Dena excitedly as they got closer.

'Yes, probably.'

'What do you mean, *probably*!'

They studied the crop circle as it spiralled along, appearing to rotate like a wheel as they drove past. There was another circle a few miles on. Dena was just as excited as the first time. Dena's eyes were wide, Hugo's were on the road.

The next field had a circle too, and the one after that. And another one a mile later. All different designs; creative, inventive, impossibly mathematical. Dena stared at them. 'I suppose not all of them are genuine, are they?'

'Oh for heaven's sake, Dena,' said Hugo, irritably fiddling with the fan blower. Little strands of straw were blowing in his face. 'Of course they're not genuine.'

Dena pursed her lips. 'Well,' she said, 'some of them might be. I mean you *want* to believe in them. It would be wonderful if they were real.'

'Even if there *are* aliens floating about up there, and of course there aren't,' (he added parenthetically) 'do you think they haven't got anything better to do than hang around in Wiltshire forming crop circles? I know I have.'

'Well – they're messages, aren't they. Messages to humanity.'

Hugo sniffed and ran a hand across his sweating forehead. 'Why can't we understand them then? Why don't they make sense to us?'

'Well,' said Dena, her forehead hurting from the concentration, 'we're not as sophisticated and intelligent as them.'

Hugo smiled. 'In that case,' he said, feeling as if he had a hotel on Mayfair and Dena had just landed on it, 'if they're so much more intelligent than us, why don't they write the messages out in English?'

Dena pulled a face and looked out of the window. She looked at her crop circles with wonder.

A small black dot appeared in Hugo's overhead mirror. It got larger, turning into a large black insect. It got bigger still, its blackness turning into green as it mutated from an insect into a something squat and reptilian.

The car got larger and quickly came up behind Hugo. The road ahead of them sloped up until a few hundred yards ahead, it reached the brow of a hill, the other side of which could not be seen.

Dena, without mirrors, was unaware of the green car. The

noise of the wind, because of the windows being down, disguised the sound of the other car. The offside wing mirror had been lost long ago, in a skirmish with an articulated lorry on the North Circular. Hugo glanced up. 'What kind of speed is he doing?' he murmured.

The car, spotted with brown rust like a toad, bore down on Hugo and for a second he looked into the eyes of the driver. He was seventeen or eighteen, with long hair flopping over his eyes and an expression of what Hugo could only describe as hate. Why did the boy hate him? What had he done? Hugo pulled his gaze away and looked back at the road.

At the point where the green car was right behind Hugo and could get no closer, the front of the car disappearing from view and Hugo having the uncomfortable, prickling feeling that the car was clinging to his back – it swerved out and overtook Hugo with a roar like a motorcycle. For a moment Hugo heard the thumping, toneless music emerging from the passenger window. Dena put her hands over her ears. Hugo was almost at the brow of the hill; the other car stayed parallel as it laboured to ascend. Hugo automatically slowed, but the other car was slowing too. Instead of dropping behind Hugo, it stayed alongside as they reached the top of the hill. The boy looked at Hugo with fury. Hugo braked. As they passed over the top of the hill Hugo looked down into the opening valley. The green car shot in front of him, its wheels practically flying off the hot tarmac, just as another startled car drove up the hill on the other side.

The green car moved back in front of Hugo with almost no space to spare and for a moment Hugo was confronted with the huge green rear, its unfriendly red lights glaring from the sickly rust mottled boot. Hugo pressed harder on the brake, the green car sprang ahead and on the other side of the road the startled third party weaved drunkenly as it tried to regain control, having braked sharply.

Hugo and Dena looked silently towards the new horizon. The

green car got rapidly smaller and smaller, mutating back into a black insect, then a dot, then disappearing in a blink. Hugo drove along in silence touching sixty, as if feeling guilty for going too slowly. Why had the young driver felt it necessary to go so fast? Why had he looked at Hugo with such an expression of utter contempt? Why, when it was obvious he could not overtake, did he not drop back?

It got hotter and hotter. Hugo squinted as the road shimmered in front of him. The heat was mesmerising. Hugo's questions buzzed round his head as he turned the car off onto a smaller, thankfully less huge, road towards Stonend.

IV

They passed through several outlying stones on the way into the circle. Lone, guard stones crouching ominously in fields surrounding the little road, the guardians of an inner circle.

The stones were in control; the road had to weave awkwardly to make its way round them, and the cars were smaller than the stones. How different to the journey, where the roads were cut where the cars wanted to go and the fields had no say in the matter.

To Hugo's surprise they found the house easily. The road took them, eventually and in its own time, right up to the door. There was a kind of island in one of the fields and the little cottage stood on this island. Hugo felt rather conspicuous as he parked the car and backed it up so they would not have far to carry everything.

Yasmina stood framed in the doorway. She had watched the car chug round the corners and gradually get nearer and nearer her house, going out of sight and then emerging like a steam train in a cartoon disappearing behind mountains and reappearing much larger. When the car pottered up the drive, she slipped back into the house and left the door open. She listened to Hugo and Dena midway through a conversation as they got out of the car.

'... never known anything like it. Look at me, I'm dripping. Look under my arms.'

'I don't want to look under your arms.'

'It's ridiculous, look where you've braked, there's black rubber from the tyres stuck to the driveway.'

'Good grief, yes, I didn't even brake particularly sharply.'

'Well you can't anyway, can you, we're going to have to do something about this car.'

'Oh, they go on for ever these old Volvos, I wouldn't change it for the world.'

'Look, the door's open, do you think we should just go in, or knock? Have you got everything?'

'You can't knock and stand there when the door's open. We'll come back for most of the stuff.'

'Where is she? Do you suppose she's in the garden?'

'What garden, I shouldn't think she's got a garden. The house looks like it's been dropped in the middle of the circle by magic. Or perhaps it landed from outer space.'

They waited uncertainly for a few moments.

'This is silly,' said Dena, eventually marching in and calling 'Yasmina,' in a loud, ringing voice. Her voice sounded throughout the house, only answered by its own echoes. Hugo followed uncertainly. He stopped in the hallway and looked at the Indian prints on the wall. There was a fat smiling Buddha made of polished wood by the telephone, and two large ceramic elephants guarding the doorway.

Various clocks ticked and chimed as they walked through the house. The furniture in each room was dark, muted and old; mahogany tables and chests, rosewood chairs with deep red seats, black beams and low ceilings. There were dark blue and purple throws over the sofas and blue rugs with intricate designs. To Hugo it seemed raffish and unkempt; to Dena it was beautiful. The windows were small and let little light in; the blazing sunshine did not manage to brighten the gloom.

Dena turned the handle of another room. They both squinted as a vast shaft of light fell over them. Irradiated, they stumbled into the room. Yasmina was standing by the windows, which reached the floor, and was looking out onto the vast, endless field of stones behind her. She wore a red dress, thick as velvet. Dena gave a little girlish squeal when she noticed Yasmina. Hugo suddenly saw his wife as she must have looked twenty years ago during netball. Yasmina and Dena hugged and Dena started jabbering away incoherently. Anyone would have imagined they were long lost sisters. Hugo closed his eyes momentarily, realising for the first time how long and awful the next few days would be.

'So this is your house? It's lovely. You always did have good taste. What a lovely dress, what's it made of, it matches the curtains, are you camouflaged? You were right about finding the house, it was no problem at all!'

Yasmina motioned Hugo and Dena towards two chairs that were placed in the middle of the room. Hugo sat down. 'Oh yes,' Yasmina was saying. 'This house is inevitable, you can't help coming to it. Even if you try.'

Dena laughed. Yasmina kissed her on the cheek, then moved towards Hugo and after a momentary pause, bent down and kissed him on the cheek too.

'I must make you some tea,' said Yasmina. 'That's what you're supposed to do when you have visitors, isn't it?'

V

'It's a beautiful home,' said Dena, looking round. 'And how won-

derful to live inside a stone circle. You must feel terribly protected, with your big stone soldiers outside on constant guard.'

Yasmina smiled. 'I suppose you're right. I'd never quite seen
it like that. Anyway, they're not all soldiers. The tall thin ones are
supposed to be male, but the squat fat ones are female.'

'Obviously a man who came up with that one!' laughed Dena.

'You've lost weight, actually, haven't you?' said Yasmina. It
was supposed to be flattering but to Hugo it sounded like surprise. He narrowed his eyes and sipped at his tea as she spoke.

Dena was not offended. 'How many stones are there?' she
asked, leaning forward enthusiastically.

Yasmina put her tea down. A waft of it reached Hugo's nose.
It was a sweetish, noxious herbal kind of tea; heaven knew what
she put in it. Manure, perhaps. Hugo could see the cup from
where he was sitting; the liquid inside it was dark green.

'Well it's funny you should say that,' said Yasmina.

'?'

'Nobody's quite sure how many stones there are.'

'Oh, surely someone's counted them.'

'Oh yes, people have counted them. But no one ever comes
to the same total.' Hugo drank some tea and grimaced.

'Yes, you see there are so many of the stones, and they're dotted around over such a large area – ' Yasmina broke off to look
out of the window and stare at one particularly large stone that
was positioned like a sentry in the field beyond the house – 'that
it's difficult to add them up properly. You end up counting the
same stone twice, or you miss some out, or – well – ' she
shrugged – 'there have been proper surveyors here, but no one's
ever got it right.'

'Can't you do it from a helicopter?'

Yasmina shrugged again. 'Different surveyors go up in different helicopters – still come back with different totals.'

'So what's the explanation?'

Yasmina studied Dena and said nothing. Slowly, lazily, she

moved her hooded eyes and looked at Hugo. He felt her gaze and involuntarily wriggled, as if his skin was being pierced by the fangs of a snake. The sensation passed; he scratched his arms and shook. As when people say someone is walking over their grave, he experienced a prickly feeling like pins and needles, then a moment later felt fine.

Yasmina was looking at Dena again. 'Perhaps you two can come up with some theories,' she said. She smiled radiantly and stood up. Her long red dress spilled from her like lava from a volcano. Hugo watched its swirls and folds tumble about her bare feet and eventually settle. 'Would you like some more tea?' she asked. 'Perhaps you'd like more of my jojoba tea?'

'PG for me thanks,' Hugo said. Yasmina took the cups and floated from the room.

'That's a bit of a mystery, isn't it?' said Dena. 'I wonder what the reason is?'

'She's just making it so, muttered Hugo. 'It's a load of mystical nonsense. You can make anything seem spooky if you want to.'

Dena raised her eyebrows at him.

'Just because a bunch of scientists disagree about something, doesn't mean there's alien involvement or a cover-up. Which is what she obviously wants us to start thinking. And perhaps there isn't any disagreement anyway. People round here, they invent mysteries. They like believing in them so they see what they want to see. Like seeing figures in the dark, or shapes in the clouds. Doesn't mean there's actually anything *there.*'

Dena pursed her lips. 'You believe in God,' she said.

Yasmina walked back in with three new cups of tea. Hugo, his face frozen in an open-mouthed expression, looked like an Easter Island statue. Dena took her tea and stirred it thoughtfully. Yasmina put Hugo's tea on the side table for him and sprawled in her chair like a voluptuous red heron settling on water.

'So,' she said, apparently unaware of the silence that had fallen like snow, 'do you want to know what the truth is?'

'Oh yes please,' said Dena.

Yasmina gazed at Dena, then at Hugo, then back at Dena again. Hugo looked at her curiously, trying to show total disinterest but failing.

'Well,' said Yasmina, clearing her throat. Dena looked at her expectantly.

'The stones move.'

She looked at Hugo, then at Yasmina. Both looked back at her expressionlessly.

'Move?' said Hugo eventually.

Yasmina nodded. 'They walk. It's well documented.'

Hugo looked away, trying not to smile. He tried to find something of interest to look at and eventually studied his cup of tea. The cup was a strange, bronze thing. It had designs around the rim; a kind of Greek patterning. Hugo drank and listened as Yasmina rambled away and his wife, wide-eyed and gullible, lapped it all up like a puppy.

Later, putting his clothes away upstairs, Hugo continued a largely one-sided conversation with Dena. The floor creaked each time he moved across it, en route for the wardrobe. 'I mean those crop circles on the way down,' he said.

'Yes?'

'Prime example. Why are there so many crop circles down here? You can drive around the whole country; nothing. Then as soon as you hit Wiltshire, bang. They're in every field.'

'That's because there's lots of fields here. We don't have crop circles in Garrington because there aren't any fields in Garrington.'

'No, it's not that. They have fields in Yorkshire, Wales, everywhere. They're not plagued with crop circles. The reason there are loads of them down here is that there no one has anything else to do.'

'Oh *Hugo*,' she said tetchily, rubbing her arm.

'Look at those huge, open roads. No villages for miles. Farmhouses surrounded by twenty miles of nothingness. There are teenagers and kids in those houses. Dad's busy, the kids have got nothing to do. Literally nothing, they can't even rip up cinema seats or vandalise phone boxes. So they make crop circles in the middle of the night.'

Dena shook her head despairingly. Hugo whistled as he folded his corduroy trousers neatly and put them on a shelf in the wardrobe marked 'Hats'.

VI

In the afternoon Yasmina took Dena into Devizes shopping and Hugo, claiming to have several books he urgently needed to read, stayed behind. After a few hours he felt immensely tired and decided to go for a walk to wake himself up. He crossed the road and went into the first field, but got no farther than the nearest of the stones.

Hugo touched it and felt a strange buzz, almost like electricity, run through him. He frowned. His body was hot from the heat and the stone was cold; that must be why it felt so odd. He should not be outside when it was this hot; he would get heatstroke if he was not careful.

He walked back to the house, nearly getting knocked over by a lunatic car tearing round the bend as he did so. The house was ominously quiet, haunted with Yasmina's peculiar, disconcerting aura. He shivered, ignored the strange icons and knick-knacks in the hallway, and went upstairs.

On the landing, tucked into a dark corner, was a bookcase he had not noticed before. He ran his eyes quickly over the titles. There was nothing to interest him. Several well-thumbed books on the occult, one on the end of the universe, two Agatha Christies and several battered paperbacks on Buddhism.

Only one title caught his eye sufficiently to make him pick it up and look at it. It was called *The Message to the Planet* by Iris Murdoch. Hugo had never read anything by her, vaguely assuming that all her books were about large families having arguments and sex with their wives' best friends. He picked the book up. It fell open on a particular page and a passage was marked with a wavy black line.

> The Avebury stones (being either pillars or squares) are said to be male and female symbols, suggestive of a fertility cult. It was said that in the twelfth century the incumbent at Avebury church had put a terrible curse upon the stones which were so clearly the work and abode of evil spirits. The legend was that one of the stones, distressed or incensed by this treatment, set off one night and walked to Bellmain where, it was implied, it received the protection of more friendly powers. It appeared that stories of walking stones were not uncommon, a particular stone still at Avebury was said to walk across the road at certain times, and the stones at Rollright went down to the river to drink at midsummer.

Hugo closed the book and replaced it on the shelf. He pushed it further back so it was flush with the others and didn't look as if it had been moved. Around him, the house breathed gently. Several times he imagined he could hear Yasmina's voice, although he knew Dena would not bring her back for several hours. He lay down in the bedroom for a few minutes and was soon fast asleep.

They woke Hugo for dinner; he was grouchy until Yasmina gave him some wine in a silver cup. He looked at it suspiciously before drinking it. 'Looks like a chalice,' he said. Yasmina smiled.

Hugo drank most of the bottle and was soporifically happy for the rest of the meal.

VII

Once in bed, however, Hugo could not sleep. The bed was hard and the foul green vegetable concoction that Yasmina had cooked made his stomach rumble. Dena's light, contented snoring, which usually soothed him and lulled him into sleep, merely kept him awake. He turned the pillow over to make it cooler, and punched it to make it more comfortable, but still lay there staring at the dark blue square of light behind the fraying curtains and listening to the strange country sounds that he was not used to.

'I never knew how noisy the country is', he muttered to himself. He listened to his voice bouncing from the unfamiliar ceiling. People from the country always go on about how peaceful it is, he thought, away from the traffic of the towns. But it was a total racket outside. Owls hooting, hedgehogs and foxes creeping about, twigs snapping, God knows what moving about immediately underneath his window. He turned over, and after a little while turned over again. He got out of bed, opened the curtain, squinted in the sudden light, and looked down at the blueish blackness. Trees and grass. In the middle distance, a stone shone and sparkled in the moonlight like an uncut diamond.

He listened to the sound of his own breathing. What a strange thing it is to 'have' a body. We are part of our bodies; we are our bodies. But this is an alien notion to us, somehow, even when we have inhabited our bodies for years. Even that last sentence betrays the way we see our bodies, Hugo thought. We feel that they are separate things – we talk of having a body, as if it is a thing other than what 'we' are. When you speak of 'having' a body, what is the thing that 'has' it? The brain? The mind? But these things are still part of the body.

When I die, thought Hugo, my soul goes to Heaven. But what is the soul? And – as Hugo stared down at the dim silhouette of a tree, a fear gripped him – is the mind part of the soul? What happens to my mind when I die?

Hugo clutched the curtain. It's not much use, he thought, if my soul goes to heaven but the contents of my brain – everything I think, feel, believe, doesn't. If all that vanishes – ceases to exist with the body – then what's the use of a soul going to heaven? It's not much comfort if it's just my 'spirit,' whatever that is, floating around in heaven. It won't be 'me'. He let go of the curtain, shook his head and got back into bed, closing his eyes and telling himself to go to sleep.

Most people seem to think 'they' themselves go to Heaven. If they give it any thought at all, they imagine Heaven to be much like Earth. They meet the people they loved on Earth; they think they will 'meet them again in Heaven.'

Wish fulfilment, thought Hugo. Suppose there really is a Heaven. In practice, what is it actually likely to be? It's not going to be a – he searched his mind for the word – *material* place like Earth. How can it be?

And what do you do there? Can you really take it seriously, the idea of it being a place where you pal up with old friends and family and – do what? Spend infinity talking about the good old days when we were alive? When you start to think like this, Hugo thought, believing in God begins to seem... begins to seem...

He jumped out of bed and tapped his fingers on the windowsill. The wood seemed very hard, full of texture and grain; he ran his fingers over it and marvelled at how real it seemed. He looked back at the bed; it was rolling slightly from where he had leapt out, but Dena was still sleeping peacefully, entirely undisturbed. She would not stir a muscle all night and then would jump out of bed refreshed and alert at eight o'clock; just like any other day.

Hugo opened the window and let the warm night air bathe his face. How could it be this hot, he wondered. He tried to swallow, but his mouth was too dry. He stumbled over to the door, bumping into the edge of the bed en route. He felt blindly for the handle and pushed it open. There was enough light in the hallway to see down the stairs.

In the kitchen he poured himself a glass of water and downed it in one long mouthful. He wiped the sweat from his forehead. His stomach was churning, although he was not hungry; when he thought about food it made him feel queasy.

He turned from the kitchen and heard a faint, muffled noise behind him, like something heavy being dragged across the carpet. He paused in the doorway and looked around, then glanced out of the window. Nothing visible moved. Shaking his head, he moved towards the stairs but then stopped again, trying not to breathe. There was definitely a noise coming from somewhere inside the house. Like something being scraped, or pushed. Like a heavy box being moved slowly across the floor.

He stood still, listening to his breathing. It's amazing how loud breathing is; you don't realise unless everything else is silent. He waited, heard nothing and relaxed, and moved towards the stairs. Then he heard it again. It was now lighter in tone; not as heavy. It now sounded like a cat – a kind of soft, deliberate padding; and it was coming from the direction of the stairs. Hugo hesitated for a moment. The tense silence changed tone and became a relaxed silence again; so he stepped into the hallway.

Perhaps it *was* a cat. An absent cat that came to life in the middle of the night was exactly the kind of thing Yasmina would have. A *familiar*, Hugo thought; in his intense, heightened state the thought seemed funny. He stifled an urge to laugh.

There was nothing on the staircase – no cat, no ghost. No

ghost of a cat. Hugo glanced across to the room opposite the staircase. The door was in front of him now, its multicoloured glass pattern throwing strange colours on the stone floor. The reds, blues, greens and yellows now appeared as purples, blues, greys, and somehow, illuminated blacks. Multicolours in negative, thought Hugo – as if such a thing were possible. What was the negative of a colour, he wondered. All colours are blue on a photographic negative – why is that? Anything seemed possible here.

He touched the handle; the hand seemed to be detached, not part of Hugo's body. The fingers moving individually round the handle resembled a giant spider coming to life.

The door opened silently and Hugo crept into the front room. It was pitch black; the curtains were thicker and the blue, moonlit sky did not enter here as in the other rooms. The air buzzed with silence and Hugo tried to discern the noise from the background hum. Something, anything, as a logical explanation would do.

There was nothing there, apart from the sound of his own breathing. But the breathing seemed to be coming from the other side of the room. Hugo cocked his head. Somehow he was managing to throw the sound of his own breathing. Not a knack he knew he possessed. Perhaps there was a strange configuration of the furniture, bouncing his breathing around the walls. He remembered the way his voice had echoed off the ceiling in the bedroom.

Hugo struggled to think rationally. Could his breathing be bouncing off the walls? Were his heightened senses just imagining it? There was nothing to hear so they filled in the sound for him, as his brain seemed so keen to hear something?

He ran his hand along the wall by the door for a light switch, but could not find one. He touched the wall on the other side of the door. It was bumpy, old, and cool to his hot hand. He looked away from the wall, down at the floor, while he tried to find the switch. Eventually his hand made contact with an old-fashioned, circular brass fitting. The switch was a small, thin, brass stick with a rounded end. Hugo snapped it down sharply and with a loud click, light flooded the room.

Hugo found himself looking at the familiar bare feet of Yasmina; then his eyes ran up her bare legs. She stood legs slightly apart, her arms at her sides. She wore a red bra and red knickers. Hugo swallowed uncertainly. Yasmina looked at Hugo with an open, vulnerable expression.

'What on earth are you doing creeping about in the middle of the night?' complained Hugo. He tried not to notice her large, rounded breasts rising and falling like the sea as she breathed deeply. He tried not to look down at the pale pit of her stomach, shadowed coyly by the yellow light from her side. He tried not to look at the bright red triangle below, a lick of flame thinly covering Yasmina's soft flesh. He tried not to look at the low mound that rose there, and the soft bumpy shape of Yasmina's pubic hair like the mossy grass covering a barrow.

'I could ask you the same question,' said Yasmina. She stepped towards him and Hugo watched the different parts of her body move like a machine; the thighs lifting and falling, the breasts tipping forwards and settling again, the stomach creasing and smoothing, the hair flowing onto her shoulders then falling behind her.

'What are you *doing*,' said Hugo, 'what are you up to, what is this all *about?*'

Yasmina opened her eyes wide and looked at him, as if in astonishment. Hugo made strange puffing noises while he waited for her to speak. She did not say anything.

'I mean what's going *on?* Why isn't anything *normal* here? Oh, I'm going back to bed.'

But Hugo did not move. Yasmina took another step towards him. It felt like Grandmother's footsteps, thought Hugo, with all the tension and uncomfortable feelings that game induces. He shook his head. Why was he thinking about Grandmother's footsteps, for heaven's sake?

Yasmina was standing in front of him. He could feel the warmth of her body. The tips of her breasts touched his chest. Her nose went out of focus as it got close to his face and he could feel her breath. He tried to move his head back, but found that he couldn't. She passed that invisible threshold where she came into his space. Hugo tried to step backwards. He was unable to; he felt rooted to the spot.

Yasmina raised a hand and touched Hugo's lips. Her hands were hot. She gave off a heat that was dizzying, almost nauseating. 'So what's going on,' murmured Hugo, 'I suppose I'm going to be seduced now, am I?'

Yasmina looked at him blankly.

'It's not going to work you know, my wife's upstairs, I'm not going to sleep with you.'

Yasmina shook her head, ignoring him rather than disagreeing. 'That doesn't matter,' she said.

'What do you mean, it doesn't matter?'

Yasmina smiled. 'You don't understand, do you?'

'Hmm?'

'I've seduced you already.'

'Right, I see. Rubbish.' Hugo tried to step backwards, but couldn't. He tried to lift his legs; they would not move. Yasmina came even closer to him. Impossibly close now; he felt as if she was going to merge into him.

'I have cast you under my spell.'

Hugo snorted. 'What does that mean?'

'Things won't be the same again. You'll see.' She pressed an arm against Hugo, and for a moment he had the sensation of her arm slipping right through his arm and emerging again on the other side. She slid her leg up to his groin and wrapped herself around him like a snake. She coiled into him and he felt squeezed; for a moment he couldn't breathe. He felt a stabbing, prickling pain flow up and down his body like pins and needles. He felt uncomfortably hot, as if he was about to faint.

'I have bewitched you,' she said.

He ignored her.

'I'm not who you think I am,' said Yasmina. Her voice seemed suddenly different – hollow, almost – as if she was in the bath, or inside a metal room.

'What's that supposed to mean?' Hugo said. He was irritated – irritated because it was all so stupid, but also because he felt the presence of Dena a few feet above him, and wondered if she could hear anything.

On his way up to bed, he found a red thread attached to his hand. He removed it, and dropped it on the floor as he reached the top of the staircase. He went into the bedroom, held his breath as he looked at Dena sleeping contentedly, then got in next to her.

VIII

The next morning, Dena woke up refreshed and alert, but was unable to get Hugo out of bed. He was murmuring in his sleep, creasing his face up, reaching into the air with his hands and screwing them up into fists.

Dena looked down from the window at the large semi-circle of visible stones, the scrub trees bordering the foreground and in the distance, the flat pale yellow fields. She looked at her watch. If he was not up soon, they would be late for church.

On the window sill in front of her was a random collection of pebbles. Flints, sheared on one side to reveal their glossy, silver innards like marble. Sandy coloured rounded pebbles from the beach, mottled with brown freckles like eggs. She picked up one of the pebbles and tumbled it in her hand. She turned and looked at her sleeping husband.

Eventually he vaguely woke, emerging like a whale from the waves of sheets. He groaned and muttered as if he had a headache. He was sweating and his face was pale. Dena sat on the edge of the bed and put her hand on his forehead. 'Are you all right? Have you got a fever?'

Hugo lay still and stared at her. 'Are we going home?' he said.

'It's Sunday, Hugo, we're going to church.'

He looked agitated. 'No. No, I don't want to go to church. Please. Please.' He was gaunt, worried, ill. 'Let's go home.'

'Where is she then?'

'She can't have just disappeared. It's only eight o'clock.'

Yasmina was not in bed. Her bedroom door was open and white curtains billowed from the wide open window. The room was suffused with light. As Hugo and Dena stood in awe on the threshold looking in, the room seemed to glow, pulsate.

Yasmina's bed was an ostentatious, antique pile. It was a four poster, of course, and it had red drapes, naturally, and plumped velvet pillows and white silk sheets; what else would she have, Hugo thought. If he had given any conscious thought to the kind of bed Yasmina might have owned, this would have been the picture his mind might have conjured. And here it was. There were gargoyles engraved on the bed heads and the posts were carved to appear plaited.

Hugo could not actually visualise her sleeping on it. He could imagine her levitating a foot or so above its surface, or worshipping some pagan deity at its foot. But he could not conceive of Yasmina doing anything as mundane as sleeping.

I've seen the bed she owns – the bed she *possesses*, he thought, his mind strangely advancing mystical puns all of a sudden. He shook his head and turned wildly to look at Dena. 'Well – she can't have got far,' he muttered. 'We'll look for her.'

The house appeared to be empty, although there were windows open in every room. The dark gloominess of the house that had so struck Hugo on his arrival had completely disappeared. Swept away by light, the house now radiated warmth and energy. It was as if Yasmina had ascended, or vaporised. Hugo kept these thoughts to himself.

Dena squinted and held a hand over her eyes when she went into the kitchen and called Yasmina's name. She turned back to Hugo with a bemused expression. 'She's definitely not here,' she declared.

IX

They wrote a note to Yasmina after spending some time debating exactly what should and should not be written. They screwed the note up and wrote another one, then another. Hugo did not want it to be too long-winded and ponderous; Dena did not want it to be too casual and flippant. Eventually they agreed that all that was needed was a fabrication about having to get back, in order to prevent their sudden departure seeming too abrupt, and a promise to get in touch soon. They both signed it. Dena added two kisses. 'Right,' said Hugo. 'Come on, let's go.'

They threw their possessions in the back of the car.

'I'll drive,' said Dena.

Hugo looked at her. 'Okay.'

She had to start it three times. She turned the key with her lips pursed.

'It's the heat,' defended Hugo. 'It doesn't like it, poor thing, neither do I. Give it a bit more rev. Don't rev it too much, you'll flood it.'

Dena shot him a look.

'Sorry,' he said. 'Turn it off and leave it for a minute.' The car ticked like a clock as they sat in silence waiting for it to work; she revved it again, but it still refused to go. Dena rubbed her face with her hands; when she removed her fingers there were red marks on her face.

Hugo watched as Dena got frustrated. What was she really thinking? What did she think of Yasmina? Did she really like her as much as she appeared to? What did she think of Yasmina's odd ideas about walking stones? What did Dena really *think*? What went on in her mind? Hugo did not really know. It's amazing how you can be married to someone for years and believe you know them so well – there isn't a single opinion they hold or feeling they feel that you don't know inside out – and yet you don't really know them at all.

The car eventually pulled away, over the slight hump of tarmac that created Yasmina's island, and bumped down the road. Hugo heard the exhaust pipe scrape the gravel and he winced. Dena drove past the fence separating the road from the field, both hands gripping the wheel intently. Hugo watched the stones flash past. The tall, columnar stone that was apparently male. The diamond shaped squat stone in the opposite field that was apparently female. Hugo sighed and shook his head.

'Are you all right?' asked Dena.

'Mmm. Just thinking.'

'Thinking about what?'

Hugo shook his head again. He looked out of the window. The grass seemed particularly green in the field opposite. They were approaching two guard stones, the ones Hugo had thought looked ominous and portentous when they arrived. Hugo started to smile. He was pleased to be finally escaping the place. He could already feel the temperature starting to drop. It would get cooler, and soon he would be home and stretching his feet out in the garden and sipping a glass of wine and feeling serene and calm, and free from crazy women who claimed to bewitch and enchant him.

They passed the stones. Hugo's smile froze on his face.

There was another stone.

He was not imagining it. The stone had not been there before. Coming from the opposite direction, the two guard stones were the first he had seen. They were the first that were there. He knew that, because he had been so struck by them when he saw them. So if they had been the first, where had this one come from?

It was a squat, squareish stone, with blunted corners. A female stone. Hugo felt, as if from a distance, a strange sound forming in his throat, guttural and primitive. His throat was separate from him. His arm involuntarily and ineffectually slapped against the window. His body seemed to depart from him and float away. He was somewhere else, he was removed from his flesh.

Dena drove nearer to the stone, then parallel to it. It seemed to stare at Hugo, observe him, watch him. It seemed to have its arms folded, it seemed to be looking at him with raised eyebrows. Hugo tried to cry out, but no sound came from his mouth.

He looked closely at the stone as the car juddered along. It was close now, just a couple of feet away, and he could see it in all its ominous impressiveness.

There was a piece of red thread attached to the stone, about halfway down. Bright red. Under a kind of crevice, a kind of dip in the stone, at the front. Hugo spluttered, tried to speak, couldn't.

Nothing would be the same again; he suddenly felt that clearly and strongly. The stone looked at him. It seemed to leer, to wink. The car drove on mercilessly. Hugo craned round in his seat and looked behind him. The stone, that last week had not existed, was there. It was as real as him. Realer. He thought of helicopters and scientists and stones, and rivers at midsummer. The thoughts in his mind merged and blurred, and congealed, and locked.

Hugo felt his spine contract and his eyes seemed to bulge. His head pulsated, as if he was staring at a strong, bright light. He could feel the veins leaping from his forehead. His hands started to shake uncontrollably and his body slipped and skidded like an eel under the grip of the seatbelt. The picture went negative – a black stone against a grey background – and then everything seemed to vanish.

The temperature got cooler on the way home. By the time Dena turned into the driveway, it was almost cold.

X

Two months later, the vicar wrote to Hugo and asked him why he had stopped coming to church. Before he signed off he wrote, 'Is it because you've seen a vision? Please do let us know if so!!'

Dena read the letter out to Hugo as she sat on the edge of his bed, but his expression did not change. She found her mind wandering while she read the letter, which rambled on in places about the preparations for Harvest Festival and the fund to raise money for the restoration of the spire. After giving Hugo his breakfast she answered the letter, with cheerful exclamations on the part of Hugo. She claimed in it that she still had hope he might be able to respond to his own letters in the future.

'I'm going down to see Yasmina again at the weekend,' she told him. 'She says it's very hot down there. She's told me to bring my bikini, she says we'll sit in the circle and lie on the stones. That's what everyone's doing down there at the moment, apparently. Sounds nice, doesn't it? Just lying out in the sun all day, enjoying the world. You don't have to worry, the nurse will drop in to see you.'

She was comfortable now with talking in a monologue; talking to Hugo as if he would respond, then carrying on – answering her own questions, talking much as one might speak to an infant. She pulled Hugo forward, plumped his pillow and pushed him back again. She absently wiped a little dribble from his mouth with the back of her hand. He looked up at her with watery eyes.

Dena checked her watch. She looked after Hugo with a certain briskness, and never let herself become too sentimental or maudlin. She still had a faint hope that he would get better. After all, these things are not set in stone, and Hugo wouldn't want her to be upset and ruin her life by feeling she had to stay in all the time and look after him.

She hummed to herself as she went downstairs, checked her hair in the mirror and found her handbag. She took the keys outside and pointed them at the Audi, shaking her head as she always did when she remembered how much money Hugo had kept lying around in his account. She locked the door behind her.

From his bed Hugo could move his eyes and see her. She drove away into the light. He listened to the sound of his own breathing. Later that evening, the sun slowly set. Hugo looked longingly at the glass of water on the table next to him, and wondered how long it would be before Dena put it to his lips.

la belle époque

I

The hotel presented itself to the outside world as a haven of refined elegance, but the thick red curtains were frayed and the plush fittings ragged. The ghosts of eighty or ninety years of long-dead people made the ceilings yellow and the brass doorknobs dull, and the spidery cracks in the walls dance like lines on a skull.

Steven and Natalie descended in the lift, gazing at themselves in the mirrors that flashed past on the walls, visible from behind the glass door. The glimpses of reflection, like the image captured in the split second when a camera shutter opens and closes, showed two young people of different heights, weights, age, colouring, sexes.

The black wiry cables behind them groaned and the lift shuddered to a halt. Steven swallowed. 'Always makes my ears pop when it does that.' The lift doors opened silently, glossily, with that slightly insolent, condescending air that glass doors have. There was a tired smell of wood polish in the lobby. Natalie followed Steven from the lift and they walked past the piano that was never played and the crisp newspapers that were never read. In a pot, a plant that was never watered wilted.

They walked past reception and nodded at the two young, beautiful girls. The blonder of the girls nodded at Steven. 'Good afternoon,' she said in a heavy French accent. The other girl smiled. 'Good afternoon,' she said, in a mirror of her friend's accent. They both nodded their heads and gave a kind of curtsey as they said it.

Steven smiled back, opened his mouth to think of something to say, then gave up and smiled again. Natalie took his arm and led him towards the door. They left the hotel without a sound, their footsteps adding imperceptibly to the gradual, inevitable wear. Beneath their feet the carpets were slowly thinning, like a man past the prime of life, refusing to believe he was gradually going bald.

II

Outside, the plate glass windows shimmered yellow from the hot, setting sun. They walked past the métro and the little glass pyramid; it was like a miniature version of the Louvre pyramid, or one drawn by a child. The struts between the triangular panes of glass were plastic and dirty. Bird shit obscured much of the glass near the apex.

Steven chose the restaurant. They settled in their seats and Steven studied the wine list the waiter had given him. 'Look at this,' he said. 'A bottle of '98 Fleurie, for eight pounds. That can't be right, surely. Twelve euros; that is eight quid, isn't it?'

Natalie was still taking her coat off. She had got her arm caught in one of the sleeves and was trying to tug it through without damaging the fur cuffs. 'I can't get my coat off,' she said helplessly, pouting like a child. Steven watched her struggling. 'Well if it didn't have those silly fluffy bits all over it,' he murmured, as he got up and helped her remove it. He hung it on the back of her chair. 'Let's hope no passing hunter takes a pot shot at it,' he added, sitting down again. She stuck her lower lip out at him, then closed her eyes when he reached across the table and kissed her on the cheek. 'Purr,' she said, keeping her eyes closed and wrinkling her nose and pushing her face up. 'Purr.'

'So, er, I was saying...' he said, 'Twelve euros is about eight pounds, isn't it?'

'I don't really know.'

'I told you, just think of it as dollars.'

'Well it is then.'

'Well I don't think that can be right.'

'Oh. Perhaps it's a misprint.'

'The menu's written by hand.'

'Well I really don't know, darling.' She spread the palms of her hands out and examined her nails. 'I don't know, perhaps it's because it's so old. It might have gone off.'

He narrowed his eyes at her and rubbed his lip with his finger. Perhaps she does it deliberately, he thought. 'Perhaps,' he said, 'Fleurie is, I don't know, a *district* or something, and we just know Fleurie to be a particular type of wine from that area that's really expensive.' He tapped the menu. 'But that won't be this.'

When the waiter came over he ordered it. The waiter straightened up and looked at him, and nodded. 'Bon,' he said, 'vous aimez votre vins, je sais.' He looked at Steven with an apparently new respect.

'What did he say?'

Steven frowned. 'I don't know, he said it too quickly. I just nodded and smiled.'

'That always works.'

The Fleurie arrived and the waiter showed it to Steven, who nodded approvingly. 'In a supermarket that would be fifteen, twenty pounds,' said Steven, leaning towards Natalie as the waiter uncorked the wine. 'In a restaurant it would be thirty. We get ripped off in England, you know.'

'Yes, I suppose we do.'

Steven tasted the wine and nodded, and the waiter filled the glasses up. 'No *suppose* about it.'

The food was sensational, and cheap, and they were full before the pudding arrived. Natalie said she couldn't manage a sweet at all, but Steven said she had to, because it was included, so she asked for the blackcurrant sorbet, and she was glad she did because when it arrived it was delicious, and Steven kept wanting to try it, and she found she could eat all of it without feeling any more full, and Steven had apple tart and could barely finish it.

'Well I enjoyed that tart,' he said, sitting back and breathing in the smoke from a neighbouring party's cigarettes. Natalie giggled.

'I haven't enjoyed a tart as much for ages.'

She shook her head and put her hand over her eyes.

Somewhat drunk, Steven stood in the toilets and swayed. The walls were covered on all sides with mirrors. Steven gazed at himself, gazing at the back of himself in the mirror behind him, gazing at a side view of himself somewhere within the mirror within the mirror.

The bill arrived. Natalie took one look at it and quickly paid it. When Steven came back she looked at him innocently and said that the waiter had come with the bill so she had decided just to pay it there and then.

'But I said I'd pay for it.'

'Well it doesn't matter, it can be my treat.'

'Did you leave a tip? Was service included?'

'Well – I don't know.'

'Didn't you ask?'

'Well – um… I don't know what it is in French.'

'Well it says *service compris* at the bottom of the bill, if it is.'

'Well I didn't know that.'

He poured the rest of the wine into his glass and shook his head thoughtfully.

Don't mention it, Natalie thought.

Outside the sky was yellow and sulphurous. Natalie picked at her clothes and held her hand out, and watched as sweat gathered in the palm. Steven followed her out of the restaurant. 'There's going to be a storm,' he murmured. Natalie looked upwards as they walked back to the hotel. The wing of a plane caught the sun and gleamed for a moment like a wielded spear.

They walked past the pyramid and glanced at sky the colour of a dying light bulb reflected in its panes. They could see the road either side of the pyramid, and the sky appearing to be many impossible thousands of feet away inside it.

'There are too many planes in the sky,' Natalie murmured, taking care that Steven did not hear her, knowing that he would tell her off for being silly.

III

The girls were not on reception; there were dull, unfriendly young men there, who nodded at them but did not speak.

Natalie and Steven watched their reflections shimmering in the mirrors on each floor as the lift lunged upwards. It shuddered to a halt on the fourth floor and they got out. Drunkenly walking along, his feet occasionally tripping on the rumpled red carpet, Steven tried to reach out to hold on to Natalie but he misjudged it each time and she always stayed slightly ahead. She waited by the door for him.

'When we're married,' he said, aiming the key at the keyhole and stabbing it against the wood in the door, 'we'll live in a big house in the country and have five children and drink Fleurie every night.'

'Okay.'

Eventually the key went in, and he fell into the room.

She stood by the long window, pushed the drape to one side and looked down at the street far below. People hurried into the bars; chatted while putting their collars up urgently and walking away; waved goodbye before they had finished speaking. Like birds, or cows, they could sense the approaching storm. Natalie's eyes travelled upwards; above the solid buildings, the atmosphere was a thick, evil orange. She opened the window but there was no breeze. She watched globes of sweat forming from nowhere on her skin, then running down her legs and making her shiver.

'I'd like to suck your toes.' He watched her long, thin legs in the mirror, and admired her slim, firm, toned bottom. He could hardly believe she would be thirty-four in a few weeks' time. She looked seven or eight years younger.

Outside, the heat shimmered on the tarmac.

Afterwards, Steven fell asleep against Natalie's breast. Gently she slipped out from underneath him and laid his head on the pillow. She pulled the white sheet from where it lay rumpled at the foot of the bed and laid it over him. In his sleep he frowned, turned over and pushed the sheet away from him.

Natalie slipped quietly out into the corridor. She walked along to the archway, running her hand along the wall. She turned into the alcove, walked past the lift, and stood at the top of the stairs.

She walked back to the room and went inside. Closing her eyes, she stepped out into the corridor again. Still with her eyes shut, she touched the wall, and started walking alongside it. She counted, out loud, up to six, turned to her left, walked another five steps forward, turned left, felt out with her right hand for the wall, and opened her eyes. She was at the top of the stairs. Nodding to herself, she walked back to the hotel room and closed the door behind her.

Slipping out of her clothes, she left her bra and knickers on and got into bed. Steven slept soundly next to her, snoring slightly.

Outside, the rain started to ease off.

IV

Lightning did not strike the hotel and in the morning, Natalie awoke to a fresh-smelling, beautiful day. While Steven slept, she got out of bed and stood by the long window. Far below her, the street glistened grey and wet. The sun rose lazily, a pale egg yolk colour as if with a hangover from the storm, above the silhouettes of square, metal buildings.

Natalie watched as people entered the shops, then came out with newspapers and baguettes under their arms. One elderly eccentric shuffled slowly into the florists' with a huge bunch of red roses, emerging a few moments later with an equally huge bunch of yellow ones. Natalie lit a cigarette.

She watched the smoke waft over the balcony, excitably making its mind up whether to travel upwards or downwards, with never a glance back to its parent cigarette, before it blissfully vaporised in the eternal, enormous air.

After breakfast, Steven wanted to go to the *Musée des Beaux Arts*, but Natalie was insistent. 'Oh please let us go to the market, please, please.' She tugged at his arm like a child. He smiled and gave in to her, as he always did when she was cute and endearing. 'Yes, all right,' he said, 'we'll go to the market if it's so important to you.'

She skipped along the street like a girl, her hair flopping in the wind. She insisted on leading the way, even though Steven said she would get them lost. She studied the map intently, double- and triple-checking each time they went into the métro where they were going, making sure they got the right line, and continually studying the map on the way to make sure they were still going the right way. She counted off the stations as they passed and when they reached Wazemmes, she leapt up. 'There you are,' she said triumphantly. 'You have no faith in me!'

Outside Steven adjusted his hat and Natalie led the way, until she read a signpost wrongly and he had to guide her back in the right direction.

Wazemmes market was exotic and huge. They walked round a set of stalls in the market square, and Natalie bought an orange candle with a scent so strong that later on, Steven could smell it in her bag. They spent half an hour walking round, thinking that they had covered the entirety of the market, before walking into another square, four times the size of the first one, also entirely filled with tents. At this point, Steven abandoned the methodical route he had been following to enable Natalie to visit all the stalls without unnecessary backtracking; now, they just wandered idly through and stopped at anything that interested them.

Beyond the market, they walked through the town. The cultural mix of people was much more interesting than in the main part of Lille; these were people who actually lived and worked here, as opposed to tourists and the well-off.

'I'm just going into this beauty shop for a moment,' said Natalie, before disappearing through a plate-glass window as suddenly and unexpectedly as Jean Marais through the mirror in *Orphée*.

He waited outside, leant against a pavement railing and watched people go by. Two huge women in Ghanaian dress, brightly coloured, swirling silk patterns, a matching, wrapping turban, stood outside a shop and chatted. A quartet played jazz; three of them were average and plodding but the saxophonist was superb, and a showman too, dancing enthusiastically towards anyone who approached, nodding at people he knew, trying to communicate with his eyebrows because he couldn't take his mouth or hands away from the instrument. Steven watched him and eventually the man started waving at him, dancing exaggeratedly and pointing to the hat that lay on the pavement in front of him. Steven turned his back and leant the opposite way on the pavement railing.

On this pavement sat an East European woman – Romanian perhaps, or Albanian. She had an expression of utter misery on her face. She sat cross-legged, clutching an empty paper cup, and looking around mournfully from time to time. She had a printed headscarf around her grey, straggly hair, a bright red cardigan and a thin, dirty wraparound skirt. She resembled a woman of 55 but her eyes were relatively dark and bright, and still inquisitive; perhaps she was no more than 40. People hurried by on their way to the market, and men in suits moved quickly past her on their way back to work from lunch. Steven waited for another ten or fifteen minutes outside the shop. No one put anything in the woman's paper cup.

He watched as two girls, no more than eight or nine, entered the shop. They were charismatically dressed in jeans with pictures and sequins hand-sewn into the denim; they had evidently designed the clothes themselves. They looked fashionable and sophisticated, but thankfully did not feel the urge to make themselves look older than they were; their tops had cartoon characters hotfoiled into the cotton, and their hair was in pigtails. They walked hand in hand into the shop; did it sell anything other than make-up, Steven wondered. Probably not.

As he walked in to seek out Natalie he nearly tripped over a poodle which was lying in the centre of the shop. Natalie was absorbed in rows and rows of make-up. She was comparing two identical colours and calmly smiling to herself as she chose one and put the other one back on the shelf, then changed her mind and swapped them round; then changed her mind again and swapped them back for her original choice; then looked at it uncertainly as if realising that the first choice had been the right one, but unable to tell by now which was the first choice.

'Are you nearly done?' he asked, standing behind her. She did not notice him. He tapped her on the shoulder and she jumped. 'Oh, hello darling,' she said, 'I'll only be a few minutes, I'm trying to choose between these two. What do you think?' She held the identical lipsticks either side of her mouth.

He walked outside, sidestepping the poodle. The two eight-year-olds were trying out lilac lipstick on each other. Outside, Steven wandered along the road and looked in the window of an estate agent. What he saw astonished him: attractive, modern flats or small village houses for £40,000, £50,000.

'Hello,' said a voice behind him. 'Sorry I was so long, darling, I got a bit absorbed.'

'Yes, I know.' He hated the way she always said something very obvious as if she was telling him something he didn't know. It wasn't adding a fact to the situation, it was just an unnecessary comment. 'Look at this,' he said, putting his arm round her. 'This is an improvement on £110,000 for something that's falling down, isn't it? I could afford to live here.'

'Mmm,' she said, glancing blankly at the pictures. 'Look what I've bought,' she said. 'This is Lancôme, it's so much cheaper than it would have been at home. I've always been meaning to buy one of these,' – she waved a tiny, round pot at him – 'but could never really justify it to myself. It costs sixty pounds at home.' He raised an eyebrow at it; was it made of solid gold, he wondered.

'The girls will be so jealous.' Steven nodded and tried to make enthusiastic noises.

Natalie noticed one of the Ghanaian women, still standing next to the trumpeter. 'Oh that's pretty,' she said absently, gazing at the woman's dress.

They went to a café. Steven looked around. Why don't we have places like this at home, he thought. The coffee was fresh and smooth. Steven, who did not particularly enjoy coffee at home, found his mouth watering even before he tasted it. At the table next to him, a young man reading a Gilbert Sinoué novel ordered tea. His girlfriend looked around while he read. When the tea arrived, it was in a small teapot that looked like it was made out of chocolate. The man lifted the little chocolate lid and made his girlfriend laugh by pretending to eat it.

Natalie watched the café owner, haggard and tired looking, giving instructions to her obedient children, who ran around giving people coffees and taking away crumpled sugar packets and abandoned lemons. As she looked around she noticed, on the ceiling, the legs and feet of the children walking rapidly back and forth. It was like watching a film being projected upside down.

The entire ceiling was mirrored; on the bar, which descended from the ceiling, sat a teapot and a cup, magically defying gravity. The girl took the teapot from the bar; Natalie expected her to have to tug it away, as it appeared to be stuck there, but it came away lightly. The girl turned the teapot the right way up and tea poured upwards from it, sucking itself into the cup where it settled without falling back out again.

Above the door the disembodied legs and feet of people hurrying along the street outside walked across the ceiling, lifting their feet up and putting them down again. Natalie tried not to look down at the real people; she wanted to watch the impossible legs and feet. It was a much more interesting scene, like having a glimpse into a world in a different dimension, where the rules of physics were different.

Steven turned to his book. He was still struggling with *The Waves* and wanted to finish it before he got home. Natalie fell into a trance, watching her upside-down world with absorption. When Steven finished his chapter and tried to pull her back to the real world, she didn't want to come.

Walking back through the market, Steven suddenly caught sight of the Romanian woman, wandering through the stalls. This time, she was with a friend, and did not look so unhappy. She was smiling as she held up fabrics and felt them, and dropped them back again, and picked up other stuff and mauled it about.

'Look,' he said, touching Natalie's arm, 'when I was waiting for you in that shop, I saw that woman sitting outside begging. She doesn't look so desperate now.'

Natalie looked. 'It's a different woman,' she said, 'isn't it?'

'No, it's not. I studied her quite closely. It's definitely her. It's all a scam, isn't it? She sits on the street begging, then she goes into the market and buys herself stuff.'

'Well...' said Natalie, not wanting to believe him but unable to think of another solution. 'I'm sure it's not really like that.'

'What do you mean? How else can it be?' He leant forward inquisitively, crow-like. Natalie looked at the woman picking over scraps of cloth and shuddered. She didn't know why she was shuddering, and she dreaded Steven asking her. She tried to shield her body from him.

'Well,' she said helplessly, 'I don't know, I mean…'

Steven walked on impatiently. 'I've a good mind to tap her on the back and ask her what she thinks she's doing.'

Natalie followed Steven as he guided them back to the métro. She was completely lost, and the market was so huge, and she was glad she had Steven to look after her and get her to where she was supposed to be. She felt the nagging tightness that she always felt in large crowds of people; it was as if they were closing in on her, and she felt her breath becoming shorter and more rapid. She just wanted to get away from it, and not be surrounded by people. Even though she was outside, the air felt thick and cloying when she tried to breathe deeply and not think of all the thousands of people around her.

Well, thought Natalie, if I was begging on the streets, I would still need to buy food, and drink, and perhaps clothes if I had a child; and the cheapest place to buy these things would be a weekend market. So it did not seem incongruous to find this woman wandering around in the market, buying things.

And Steven found it interesting that the woman was smiling now, whereas before she had looked distraught, as if that was further evidence of deception. It was as if he had seized on it to prove something to himself that he wanted to believe because otherwise he felt guilty. But, reasoned Natalie, walking through the market is probably the highlight of her week. It would make me smile, she thought, touching nice things and moving through nice stalls, even if I didn't buy any of it, compared to the morning sat outside a shop begging and no one putting anything in my cup. That would make me sit there with an unhappy expression on my face.

But Natalie knew she would not be able to express any of these feelings to Steven; he would dismiss them as feeble-mind-ed or naïve. And Steven was always right. He was striding on ahead, pursing his lips as he looked around, ignoring the sausages, oil lamps and cheap knickers that swung above his head, mauled by the hands of people rummaging around him. These things were invisible to him, the heads and hands below his line of vision, as he gazed above them and shielded his eyes from the light and gained his bearings. He set off again, and Natalie followed him.

Walking along a side street that Steven believed would lead to the métro, they walked past huge steel skips that stank of rotting food. Traders from the market carried large crates of waste and rubbish on their shoulders, tipped the rubbish over into the skips and shook them out. They peered into the crates and when they were satisfied they where empty, wiped their hands on their white pinnies and walked back to the market.

Behind the skips, men and women slowly emerged. Natalie did not notice them at first, camouflaged as they mostly were in greys and browns, merging into the stone walls behind. They appeared when the traders had gone and rifled through the empty pallets and green cardboard trays.

As she walked past, Natalie noticed the Romanian woman, who was extracting a huge slice of over-ripe watermelon from between some black plastic bin liners that were splitting and spilling something yellowish and foul-smelling into the skip. The woman passed a piece of watermelon to her friend, then took out another slice for herself.

Natalie called out to Steven, but he was way ahead, consulting his map, glancing back at her from time to time, wondering why she was dawdling. Natalie trotted after him but over her shoulder, saw the woman holding the watermelon in both hands and biting into it, and bright red juice and pips running down her chin and onto her thin printed dress.

V

They went back to the same restaurant as the night before. Steven had wanted to find somewhere different, but Natalie knew what that meant; it meant trailing round streets and streets looking for a restaurant that was as good as the night before, and ending up in the same one anyway. Natalie argued that where they were last night was very reasonable and they knew they could get a really good three-course meal for €18; Steven, realising that tonight he would definitely be paying, agreed without argument.

Surprised at how easily he gave in, Natalie was happy and bubbly as they arrived and were sat at the same table. The proprietor recognised them and beamed broadly. On the table opposite were two French couples, nearing the end of their first course. In the centre of the table was a silver dish, piled high with prawns, stuffed crab claws, mussels, and other fruits de mer. The couples were picking over the remains, holding bits of claw and shell as devices to wave around and argue points rather than to eat.

'We could have their leftovers,' Steven declared, 'there would be enough for us there to make a meal.'

'Someone should do that at home,' Natalie said. 'What's the problem with running restaurants at home, why do people not go to restaurants? Because they're so expensive,' she continued, without leaving him a pause to reply in. 'So what you do is, you have a Leftovers meal. There's no menu, because of course it depends on what's left over. You just ask for the Leftovers meal, call it four quid, and you could have your plate *piled* with stuff. And everyone would be satisfied, because the restaurant would still make money as it's stuff they would otherwise throw away; and they would fill the restaurant with more people because people who wouldn't normally come in, would come in.'

'Of course,' said Steven, 'it would never take off because

everyone would come in and ask for leftovers, so there would be no leftovers because no one would have bought the meals in the first place.'

Natalie thought about this. 'No,' she agreed desolately, 'I suppose not.'

They went back to the same bar. 'We should always go somewhere different each night,' Steven complained. But Natalie wanted to go back to the same place because it was under cover – it had a kind of large plastic tent, styled like a conservatory, and it was warm and the waiters were friendly.

'I expect the waiters in the other bars would be friendly, if we ever went there to find out,' he replied.

When they ran out of things to say to each other they read their books. Natalie remembered what she loved about Steven; she had been forgetting recently. What she loved was that he didn't mind doing things like sitting in bars and reading books.

He couldn't concentrate on *The Waves*; he put it down on the table in front of him. He noticed a girl who had quietly entered the bar and sat down in a corner on her own. She was beautiful – high French cheekbones, mournful, dark brown eyes and long glistening blonde hair, as perfectly wound as a croissant.

The waiter was on his way to the bar but backtracked when he saw her. Leaning over her, he asked what she wanted, nodded enthusiastically, then raised his finger as if to say it would be no time at all, and ran off. When he had gone she stared ahead, her eyes glistening.

Languorously she held a cigarette packet in front of her mouth, the lid fell down, and she drew a cigarette out with her mouth. She dropped the packet on the table without looking at it, lit the cigarette, and stared into space whilst smoking it.

Steven was amazed at how beautiful she was, how Gallic. The cigarettes she was smoking were Gauloises; the drink would probably be Pernod or Martini. He saw now that she was crying. Not with her head in her hands, not sobbing, not audible; no one had noticed she was crying. But Steven could see her looking straight ahead, eyebrows slightly raised, as huge tears forced themselves from the sides of her eyes and made their way down her cheeks, whilst she kept her head perfectly still and tried to control her lip. The cigarette rested in her hand, its blue line of smoke rising vertically into the air as if from a village chimney.

A glass of wine appeared magically in front of her, and she sipped it, and the tears continued their inexorable, inevitable voyage down her face. Steven watched her, his eyebrows folding together and his mouth partly open; he bit the side of his mouth. Watching her triggered off some deep desire inside him to cry as well. He shook his head and concentrated on his book. The words swam up and down against each other, the sentences and the words inside them meaningless.

Steven put the book down again and looked across at the girl. He wanted to go up and talk to her, ask her what was wrong, what had happened, find out if it was her boyfriend who had walked out on her, tell her that she was beautiful and that she needn't worry, she would soon find someone much nicer, she was so pretty and lovely, if he had dumped her she was better off without him, she deserved someone really nice, and someone really nice deserved her.

But he knew he would not approach her. And if he said anything to her, it would not do any good; it would not be what she needed to hear, even though it was true.

When they got up and left the bar twenty minutes later, she was still in her corner, gazing at her almost empty glass, and her eyes were red and the tears were drying on her cheeks; but she did not blink, and the universe was large and heavy and eternal around her.

VI

Because they had been drinking so early, it was barely eleven o'clock when they staggered back to the hotel. They walked past the glass pyramid; Steven looked at his reflection distorting and scattering. There were several different versions of him, all splintered, all looking in different directions. Some of them were more complete than others. He patted the pyramid.

The girls were back on reception. 'Ah, allo,' they said, and giggled. Steven smiled at them and winked. 'I missed you the other day,' he said. 'Where were you?'

'Ah, we were on ze uzzer shift, zo, zere were uzzer girls ere.'

'Yes,' said Steven, 'yes, that's what I thought had probably happened.' One of them hid her mouth behind her hand. Steven strode on ahead and pressed the button for the lift.

When it arrived he looked around impatiently to see where Natalie had got to. 'Come on,' he said, stepping back from the lift and looking towards the entrance, where Natalie was still dawdling at reception. She followed him to the lift and got in, and he pressed the round gold button with '4' in a heavy, bold black font.

The lift heaved to itself like an awakening animal, the doors slammed shut and it lurched upwards. The cables creaked and groaned more loudly than usual; or perhaps it just seemed louder because it was late. Natalie looked at the wires uncertainly. There were three thick black cables, wound in a knot around some metal poles. They looked like they would unravel easily. Natalie watched each passing floor zoom past, and the mirrors appearing and disappearing in the corridors of each floor, and shuddered.

'What's up?' said Steven, his voice thick because his tongue seemed too large for his mouth. He held her close to him.

'Nothing,' she said, shaking her head.

As they reached each ceiling she looked with wonder at the foot-thick floor, sliced off roughly at the point where the lift was built, rushing past. It didn't seem to make any sense, that the floor could just stop, sheared off at the point where the lift shaft was sunk. How was it possible, that a floor you can walk around on, could so abruptly come to an end; you could reach out and touch it; and yet it does not cave in on the floors below.

Steven got undressed and watched Natalie in the mirror. She was standing with her bottom sticking out, turning her head round to study it, to see if it had got any bigger, or any smaller. She held her breasts in her hands, and sucked her stomach in. She opened her eyes wide and gazed into the glass, checking for lines. Steven slowly took his shorts and t-shirt off, and watched her studying herself.

What she doesn't notice, because she's too obsessed with the handle of flesh she can tug from her hip and the shape of her legs under her bottom, is that, if there is anything wrong with her body, it's that her nose is too big. But because she isn't bothered by it, it's a beautiful nose, an irresistible nose. Like Joely Richardson's – it should be too big, but because she's so beautiful, and sexy, and proud of her unusual nose, it's attractive and unique.

He walked over to her and pulled her away from the mirror. Drunk, she swayed in his arms. 'I don't want sex,' she suddenly muttered, got into bed and pulled the sheet over herself.

Steven cleaned his teeth, looked out of the window at the toenail cutting moon which rose above the black night sky, then pulled the muslin curtain across. The brass rings rattled and echoed on the metal pole. They reminded Steven of the bed warmer that used to hang in his grandparents' hallway. When he was little he would reach up and tap the bed warmer with his hand, and it would bang gently against the wall and make exactly the sound the brass rings made now. Steven always worried that if he touched the warmer too strongly, the twine that was looped to a nail in the wall would leap off, and the bed warmer would crash down. His grandparents always emphasised how old it was; probably, he reflected sleepily now, no more than a hundred years or so; but aged six it had seemed an immense, mythical age.

Steven got into bed and put his arm round Natalie, but she turned away from and lay on her other side. He listened to her rhythmical breathing for a few moments, and watched the moon flickering behind the curtain, which fluttered gently in the slight breeze. The brass rings rattled to themselves.

Once she was sure he was asleep, Natalie got up. She moved silently to the door and disappeared into the corridor.

She took the lift to the first floor, checked the number she had written quickly on her hand, reached the door, took a deep breath, and knocked.

'Allo, entrez.'

When she went in, Marie was lying on the bed and on a nearby chair, Claire was reading a book. Both smoked cigarettes. The smoke drifted above their heads and circled lazily. Marie's smoke entwined flirtatiously with Claire's smoke; way above them, the combined coils hit the ceiling and merged into it, where in another eighty years' time it would have helped make the plaster even more yellow, and people not yet born would look up at it and wonder who the people were, these long-dead, silent people, who had made the ceilings so yellow. And they would wonder what these people had done, how they had lived their lives, who they had been.

Back down below the smoke, Natalie was asking Claire what she was reading. 'It's *Orlando*,' said Claire.

Marie breathed smoke through her nose and thoughtfully touched the long leaves of the plant that rested on a pile of books by her bed.

'I hate modern fiction,' she said. 'There's no subtlety about it. When people go to bed, they describe it in great detail, and you know exactly what they do, and what they don't do. I prefer reading books where you can use your imagination to guess at what they might do. I find that much more erotic.'

Natalie gazed at her silently. The comedy French accents had gone; evidently they had been for Steven's benefit. Claire closed her eyes as she breathed smoke out in front of her face, then opened them and nodded slowly, drunkenly, at Marie and Natalie. She stubbed the cigarette out firmly in the free-standing stone ashtray on her side of the bed. She put the book face down on the floor. The book was old; the pages were yellow and well-thumbed. As it lay on the floor, the pages curled round. A sliver of wood poked out from the rough paper.

The covers fell into shadow as Natalie's body blocked the light from the lamp.

Afterwards, Claire lit a cigarette and Marie smoked it.

'You two smoke a lot of cigarettes, don't you?' said Natalie. Marie nodded silently. Claire shrugged. 'Yes,' she said, 'I suppose we do.'

Marie sat up in bed and read from *Orlando*.

'The Great Frost was the most severe that has ever visited these islands. At Norwich a young country woman started to cross the road in her usual robust health and was seen by the onlookers to turn visibly to powder and be blown in a puff of dust over the roofs as the icy blast struck her at the street corner. It was commonly supposed that the great increase of rocks in some parts of Derbyshire was due to no eruption, but to the solidification of unfortunate wayfarers who had been turned literally to stone where they stood.'

Marie looked up at Natalie. There was a silence between them as they digested the imagination and the ideas.

'It's beautiful,' said Natalie. 'I always thought Virginia Woolf was boring and dull.'

'No no no,' Marie said passionately, bending the book back and running her thumbs lovingly over the rough yellow pages. 'That is what everyone in England thinks, but it is not true at all. Well, maybe *To the Lighthouse* is boring, that is the one everyone reads, but everyone must read *Orlando.*'

'All the ones Steven shows me are boring,' said Natalie dolefully. 'I tried to read one, and he said I wouldn't enjoy it and he was right. I don't think he's got *Orlando.*'

'Ah well. It is not a man's book, I don't think.'

'You mean it's not dryly intellectual enough for him,' Natalie replied bitterly. 'If it makes sense and it's exciting and has a plot, he thinks it's popular and therefore not any good. He doesn't like a book unless it gives him a headache trying to understand it.'

Marie nodded. 'You are in love with this?'

'What?' said Natalie, uncomprehendingly. Then she realised. 'Oh. Steven. Well. Yes. Well. No. I used to be. Not any more. Don't know why not. He's not any different. Must be me.'

Claire shook her head, and blew smoke into Natalie's eyes, and rubbed her arm.

'So why did you come to see us?' asked Marie.

Natalie shrugged. 'You asked me.'

'Is this the kind of thing you normally do on holiday?'

'No, of course not. I've never done this before.'

'And Steven. What would he think?'

She shrugged. 'He holds me back. I don't know what's gone wrong, why I don't love him any more. All the things I used to like about him, I hate.'

'What kind of thing?'

She tried to think. Even if she didn't get it exactly right, even if she couldn't describe exactly how she felt, it helped just to talk about it to these girls, to have a sympathetic presence. Warm, friendly people, as opposed to someone who would dissect everything she said and point out their flaws and their contradictions. *Its* flaws, its contradictions. She could hear Steven's voice correcting her. Everything is singular, so it's 'its' not 'theirs'.

'Well,' she said, shaking her head to get rid of the stream of thought, 'when we first went out I loved the fact that he's so intelligent, where I'm so silly. It used to make me feel safe and loved. Now I hate it. And the way that he always tells me what to do, and takes control. I feel stifled, claustrophobic because of that. I used to like it, I enjoyed being dependent on him. Not any more.'

VII

Steven woke up and wondered where he was. Why was the window in the wrong place, why did the room smell differently? He opened his eyes and looked at the long rectangle of light, and listened to the distant acceleration of the occasional car. Being on holiday did not make sense, it was a constantly disorienting experience.

He got out of bed and stood by the window, pulling back the drape and looking down at the street below, ethereal in blue light. A man stood staring at his reflection in a shop window. Steven looked round at the sleeping form of Natalie on the bed, her naked back emerging from the sheets, her arm draped over the side of the bed, her hand swinging slightly in the breeze.

He studied her and felt the usual surge of love, that meant that he could never leave her. As he watched her breathing out through her mouth so that her hair flopped about, and she murmured and made puffing noises in her sleep, he felt the waves of irritation and frustration that always accompanied this immense feeling of love.

Yes, she did annoy him. He couldn't stand the way she thought she was fat, even though it was blatantly obvious that she wasn't and he was forever telling her that she wasn't. He couldn't stand the rubbish she spouted to her friends. He couldn't stand her friends.

VIII

They walked into Old Lille, ambling slowly through the winding streets, not paying much attention to where they were going. For once Steven seemed content to walk aimlessly, without studying a map, without planning out a route that solved the travelling salesman's dilemma and devised an optimum balance between seeing as much as possible and getting back without wasting time on extraneous wandering.

They walked past old stone houses with brightly painted doors and brass plaques on the doors. They carried legends such as 'Francois Montefroy, Sculpteur' engraved in roman capitals with as much gravitas as if behind these doors were doctors' surgeries or vets' practices. I could live here, thought Steven as he walked past; where artists and bohemians are held in as high regard as any other member of the community. Peering through shop windows he saw wooden statues in various stages of completion; one artist's workshop had marvellous copies of Vermeer hanging in the windows. Natalie queried the wisdom of this; surely you would want to promote your own stuff? But Steven thought it was clever. They were such superb copies, they really leapt out at you as much as the originals do. So you recognise them, take an interest, and then you look in the shop. And then, because you know he's so good, you're more interested in the other stuff, the paintings and sculptures he really wants to sell you. If it were not for the Vermeers though, you would have walked past and not looked in at all.

They stood on the corner of Princess Street before turning back. Steven asked if he could take a picture of her in front of the sign.

'Why?'

'Because you're like a princess.'

'Oh,' she said, 'I'm not sure I like that. Princesses are horrible and snotty, sometimes.'

His shoulders sank. 'No, I just mean… oh, it doesn't matter.' Why was it that when he said anything nice to her, she had to take it so literally, or get it so wrong? Even when he said something as bald as 'I love you,' she would sometimes misinterpret him.

'Oh, right, I see,' she said. 'Well in that case, you may take a picture of me.' She stood on the opposite pavement to him, under the sign, and stood with one foot in front of the other and her arms held slightly out from her sides. He turned the camera on its side and took a picture. At the moment of time when the shutter opened and closed, Natalie wondered whether it would be the photo he would look at and think of her, once she had left him.

IX

They had a rest in the hotel room before going out for the evening. Steven fell asleep immediately without taking his shoes off. Natalie switched on the TV and flicked through till she found something in English, which by about channel 19 was CNN. Unfortunately there was no sound, but she watched the stories scrolling along the bottom of the screen while Larry King debated an American mass-murderer with a blubbing relative.

Natalie gasped in disbelief as she read one of the stories. She instinctively reached out and touched Steven's shoulder, but he remained asleep. In China, hailstones as large as eggs had killed fifteen people. As large as *eggs*, Natalie whispered to herself. As well as the fifteen deaths, the hospitals for miles around were struggling to cope, as they were packed with people with head injuries. Natalie shook her head. 'Hundreds of people with head injuries,' she murmured.

Imagine if that had happened in France, or England; it would have been a national headline of calamitous proportions; you would have heard of nothing else for days. But because it had happened in a remote part of China, no one took any notice of it. It was nothing but a throwaway line in an international bulletin. When Natalie returned home, she looked for stories in the leftover papers at her mum's house about the hailstorm, but there was nothing.

Steven was still asleep. They went to the same restaurant that evening and Steven drank most of the two bottles of Fleurie.

X

The breakfast room was in the basement, down wooden steps that creaked and stretched like a boat in harbour or a violin being tuned. When Steven made his way down, looking around like someone lost in a storm, Natalie was already sat at a table, halfway through a bowl of fruit, half-smiling at him as he tried to focus and get his bearings. Eventually she waved at him. He tripped as he walked towards her, confused by trying to reach out to her waving arm at the same time as changing direction with his feet. He sat down heavily opposite her and placed his elbow cautiously on the table, then rested his head on the upturned hand, like a china vase precariously balanced on a pedestal.

'I've made you some tea,' said Natalie. She smiled sweetly at him.

He nodded thankfully, unable to say anything. She poured him a cup and when he had downed it in a mouthful, was capable of pouring himself another one. He downed that too.

Vivaldi played in the background: Spring, played from invisible speakers as if energetic violinists were hiding behind the *trompe l'oeil* pictures in the arches.

He staggered to his feet, went to the table and piled a plate high with thin, curly bacon, scrambled egg, Gruyere, salami. He came back and sat down and she watched him eat.

She wanted to tell him that it was over, but knew she probably wouldn't quite get round to it. She made several valiant efforts to start, but didn't want to hurt him. Finally, whilst he was slowly, methodically eating like a cow in a field, she drew breath and forced herself to start speaking.

'When we go home…' she said, and stopped. She could not come out and say it. She would skirt round the issue, not make the issue the central thing. She also knew that this was one of the things he hated; that she could not be direct, that she hacked away at the side of things instead of chopping them down with one firm cut.

It was a fault of character. She knew that because he had told her so. But she couldn't help it. He was looking up at her questioningly. It was another of her impossible habits, the way she started a sentence and then paused and stared into space for ten minutes. What on earth was going through her mind, if anything, when she had these long vacant holidays of thought, he would wonder.

He waited patiently and eventually she came back to him. 'I think that when we go home, you should perhaps try, possibly, moving out.'

He pushed his mouth to one side. 'We've discussed this several times,' he said, 'and we always go round in circles, and we always eventually come back round to the agreement that I'll stay.'

'Yes I know,' she said patiently, but this time I do want you to move out. I mean, I just think it's, you know, I don't think it's, you know, working out us living together. You know, you're still the most important person to me, but we – we get on each others' toes.'

'No we don't,' he said irritably. 'We agreed that if we do live separately, you'll come round to me every night, or I'll come round to you. So it's pointless, it's just throwing money away. There's no point me spending £500 a month renting a flat, it's much more economical to stay as we are.'

She was tolerant, as she always was, and kept drilling on. What she needed to do was get angry, turn round and just say no; tell him it was her flat and he could get stuffed. But she was persistent in her patience, because she was trying to be kind to him. This to him was obstinate and stubborn, and laborious, because it was saying the same thing over and over and not getting anywhere.

'I would just prefer it if we lived separately, I think we would get on better.'

She was so absorbed in trying to make him agree to this, that she had forgotten that trying to get him to move out was only a cover for what she really wanted, which was for them to split up. She scratched her head and thought about this, and realised she would just have to bite the bullet and say it after all. If she got him to agree to moving out, then tried to split up with him, he would get cross because he would say, in that case what was the point in having the long conversation about moving out. If you wanted to split up, why didn't you just say you wanted to split up? And he would sigh and sit back in his chair righteously and she would feel stupid.

'Actually,' she said, 'I think it would be best if we just split up.'

'Oh,' he said, interrupting his mouthful of bacon, 'look, you always do this. Just because we're having a debate about whether or not to live together, doesn't mean we therefore have to split up, does it?' He looked at her as if they were playing chess and she had just made a particularly dim move, and he wanted her to realise just how dim a move it was, but wasn't going to help her out of it. 'Why are you always so extreme about things; just because we're in minor disagreement about living arrangements you cut your nose off to spite your face and say, oh well, let's just break up then.' He cut a piece of salami in half, balanced it on a piece of bread, and ate it, chewing thoughtfully.

She shook her head, lost in all this, opening her mouth but not finding anything to say. Somewhere, violinists enthusiastically played Summer.

Behind them three elderly women walked in, debated cautiously and in some detail about where to sit and pointed out each other several times, isn't this nice? Gradually they settled into their places. One of them seemed more dithery than the other two and had to be guided by them. 'Am I allowed egg as well as bacon?' she said. 'Am I standing at the wrong end of the queue?' The others would take it in turns to guide her by the arm.

Natalie tried again. 'I'll buy you a futon, you can go back to your father's, or … rent somewhere…'

'Oh, great. Thanks.' He drank another cup of tea. He looked at her as if expecting her to come up with all the answers, and for those answers to be only the ones he wanted.

'I know it's expensive, but as you're always saying, we live in a stupid area. Perhaps you need to move up north or something,' she waved her hand vaguely, not really knowing what the north was, but loosely understanding that it was cheap. 'You could afford to live there.'

'But I can't just… uproot and go and live somewhere else. What about all my friends. What about you. I won't see you any more.'

'Look, it's my flat. But you seem it to treat like it like it's your own.' She glared at him, cross with herself for falling over her words in her anger. She knew it was the kind of thing that made him think she was stupid. When they had met, he had found her little traits, her little ways of getting things wrong and making mistakes, endearing and cute. Nowadays, he seemed to just find her irritating and frustrating. *Just to* find her irritating and frustrating.

She shook her head, finding it unbelievable that she was correcting herself. It showed how much he had affected her. Well, she couldn't make herself change just to suit him. She would find someone else who would find her endearing.

They were standing, facing each other. Getting all that off her chest – even though it was only in her mind – made her less angry. 'You will always be my best friend,' she said.

'Will I?'

'Of course you will. You will always be very special to me.'

'How many times can I go back for coffee?' the old lady was saying with some concern.

'I don't think it matters, Betty,' replied one of the others soothingly. 'I don't think there are any rules.'

Betty frowned disapprovingly at this lack of order. 'You've got yellow juice,' she said.

'Yes.'

'Why have I got pink juice?'

'Because you asked for it. It's grapefruit.'

'Can we swap?'

'Yes, of course we can,' said the woman patiently, and swapped the drinks round. Betty nodded contentedly.

'This is nice music, isn't it? It's famous, isn't it? You hear it on the telly all the time.'

'Yes, it's Vivaldi.'

'Is he that nice chap in the white suit who sings?'

'No, there isn't any singing, is there?'

'There is when he does it.'

The violinists reached Autumn. There was no singing in it.

'Where I am going to go,' he said. 'I've got nowhere to go.'

She folded her arms and looked at him crossly. 'Yes, well that's why I haven't thrown you out before. But am I responsible for you or something?' Her eyebrows knitted together. She looked primitive, animalesque. Her heart beat furiously. 'It's not *my* fault that I can afford to live and you can't.'

'All I do is work,' he said. But he was not angry; he was just sad, reflective, stating a fact. 'And what have I got to show for it? Nothing.'

'I know,' she said, 'I know.' She leant across the table and touched his hand. 'But we can't go on like this.'

'I'll have to get a... I don't know, a different job.'

'Yes, that's a good idea.'

But he knew he would not get a different job; he didn't have the skills or the abilities, and trying to get another job was impossible anyway, he did not know how other people got other jobs. To rent a flat would cost £500 a month. He only took home £900 a month, and his bosses kept telling him that that was quite reasonable.

'I shall have to rent a room in someone's house,' he said. 'I'm not going back to my father's. If I do, I'll never leave.'

She nodded and stirred her coffee. Much as she tried to, she could not take a real interest, could not make herself concerned for him. She watched the coffee; it was fascinating, observing the shapes that it made. She just wanted to finish the conversation now. The coffee seemed to have no bottom when she slowly pushed her spoon into it. She pulled the spoon out again and looked in wonder at how silver it was against the opaque coffee.

'Yes, another job,' she said, and it was an effort to speak; she felt tired and the room felt heavy around her, even though they had only just got up. What was the point of being on holiday; would she have the energy to go and do things all day, she wondered idly. He was still talking in front of her, his face creased and angry.

The waitress came over and asked them what room number they were in. Natalie told her because Steven could never remember. The waitress moved over to the aged trio, who sat like Macbeth's witches around a cauldron of hot bacon. 'Coffee or tea?' the waitress asked desolately, the monotonous rhythm of her voice betraying how many hundreds, thousands, possibly even millions of times she had said this phrase before.

'Tea please,' said one of them, in a piercing, ringing accent, clear and slow and patronising, so that the French person would be able to understand her. 'With milk, please.' Her back was ramrod stiff and she nodded encouragingly.

The girl started to walk off, then froze in mid-pace and wheeled round. 'Oh, what room are you in?'

'Two four one,' said Betty clearly and proudly.

'No,' said one of the others urgently, raising a scaly finger, 'it's two three two.'

But the waitress had gone. 'Oh dear,' said Betty, her face crumpling, 'I was sure it was two eight one.'

'No, you said two four one.'

'And we're in – two eight two.'

'No, it's two four two.'

'No, two three two.'

'Oh dear. I wonder who's in two four one then?'

'Well,' said the other woman, breathing slowly on her tea, 'whoever it is, they won't be getting any breakfast.'

'You weren't very nice to me last night,' he said sadly.

She looked up and her countenance immediately changed. 'Wasn't I? Sorry, I didn't mean to... what did I say? I was tipsy, forgive me for being tipsy, I can't remember what it was, whatever it was I didn't mean it.'

He shook his head. 'It doesn't matter anyway.'

She seemed content with that, and didn't ask him again what it was that she had said or done.

Betty was looking around at the Monets. 'These pictures are beautiful, aren't they,' she said, gazing adoringly at the colours of the waterlilies and the purples and oranges of various Houses of Parliaments.

'Yes, they are,' agreed her neighbour.

'I wonder who they're by?' The others ignored her. She bit enthusiastically into a croissant, and jam spilt down her hairy chin.

Steven stood up; he could hardly tear his eyes away from this old woman. As he walked out along the threadbare carpets, she seemed a metaphor for the hotel itself. She did not realise how old she was, how much she was a faded shadow of what she used to be; a relic of a bygone time, that exerted fascination because she was so unusual, but had little relevance to the modern world. Steven caught sight of himself in a mirror. Hungover and in the harsh morning light, his face looked more lined than usual; there were bags under his eyes. This is what he would look like in another thirty or forty years, he realised. The quiet movement of winter played as he walked along the silent corridor to the lift.

XI

In the hotel room Natalie looked at herself in the mirror. She saw a person who was overweight with a fat bottom and saggy breasts. She held them up against her chest and looked at them, artificially pointing them slightly upwards. 'That's what I want them to be like,' she said. 'Like when I was twenty.' She let go of them and they slowly settled, like ducks landing on water, large and round and beautiful. She studied them thoughtfully.

They packed their bags in silence. 'I don't want to go out with you any more,' she said in a quiet, decisive voice. She carefully wrapped up the orange candle she had bought at the market, and he watched as she put it in one of her many bags.

'Why not?'

He wondered why she was putting the candle in the soft bag; if she put it in the hard bag it wouldn't get damaged.

'Because you always treat me like a stupid person.'

'No I don't,' he protested.

'You do. Poor stupid Natalie.'

'That isn't what I do, because if you remember – '

'And this is exactly the problem. You're so fucking analytical about everything. Everything has to be so fucking logical.'

'Okay,' he said. 'I'm sorry. I don't mean to.'

She neatly folded up her culottes and put them in her second bag. He was surprised at how she could be so angry and yet at the same time be so calm with her packing. 'You're right,' she said, 'you're always right about things… but I can't stand it. I hate it that you're always right. Why can't I be right for a change, and you be wrong?'

He thought about this. 'Well, I expect in certain situations –'

'Oh, for God's sake!' She laid a blouse gently in the bag. 'Can't you just be a bit more – emotional at times? Can't you be a bit more human?'

'Yes, I can be emotional, but that's not going to get us any-where unless we discuss this like adults –'

She banged the table in frustration. 'This is exactly what I mean!'

He winced. 'You'll damage the table.'

'And?' Her eyes blazed in fury.

'It might be valuable.' Maybe she wasn't so calm after all.

'Where am I going to go? I've got nowhere to go.'

She pursed her lips. If this had been her speaking, she thought, Steven would frown at her for repeating something she had said before.

'I know,' she agreed. 'That's why I'm leaving you. I'm sorry. My life is going in a different direction to yours.'

She lifted her bag up angrily, swung it round on her shoulder and Steven raised his hands in horror as he realised what was about to happen. The bag made contact with the mirror and it shattered. Steven watched both their reflections split into thou-sands of tiny, identical shards. The pieces of glass, all containing an image of him and her together, embedded themselves in the thinning carpet, into the dusty, cobwebbed thick curtains, and deep into the fabric of the crumbling sofa and the elegant chairs. Some even lodged themselves in the ceiling. Natalie fell forwards onto the floor to avoid the falling glass, which rained down behind her like hail.

XII

At the métro station he put his bag down and watched the esca-lator stretching away from him, forever descending, the rubber platforms going round and round eternally.

'I'm not coming with you,' he said.

She nodded, and waited for him to speak. 'I'll get a later train or something,' he murmured. 'Or whatever.'

She nodded again and without hesitation stood on the escalator. She turned to look at him, but did not say anything. She did not consciously walk away, but the escalator took her, and in a few moments she was carried out of sight.

He turned and caught sight of himself in a mirror by the exit. So this is what you look like when you've just split up with the girl you knew you were going to marry, he thought.

He walked out of the darkness into the strong sunlight and looked at the miniature glass pyramid. Lots of different versions of himself, all small and incomplete, looked back at him. He walked back to the hotel.

She stood among the cavernous, dull metal hemispheres deep within the main Lille station, waiting along with hundreds of others for the Eurostar, the wind blowing about her. She closed her eyes and felt the nervousness shoot through her. She tried to shake her head and remove the doubt; she had to go, she had to live, but she always had the same kind of fear. Eventually the metal tube rushed along the tunnel towards her and stopped with her carriage precisely in front of her. The last frisson of magic in the modern world, where you can stand at platform G and carriage G stops in front of it.

She got on the train and thought of shooting through the tunnel with millions of cubic feet of water pressing down above it. She shuddered; but stayed in her chair, and glanced at the empty place next to her, and read her book, and she went.

Back at the hotel Steven asked if he could take the room for another few days while he looked for somewhere to live. The two girls nodded and wrote in the book. Steven found it odd that they did not react to the fact that he was going to live here, or express any surprise that he had come back on his own. But the hotel was a haven of refined elegance, and nothing the guests could say or do would surprise the staff.

model

I

Fiona Clegg's current model, Jann, introduced himself at an exhibition at the Serpentine. He was a sallow-cheeked individual with long blond hair, dark eyebrows and tough Viking biceps. He wore loose sleeveless vest tops with shorts and sandals all year round; coming from Denmark, the English winters meant nothing to him. He was the kind of man that most women would have found devastatingly attractive; Fiona was frequently annoyed when he disappeared for nights out when she had been planning to spend the evening working.

But Jann would always be forgiven, because none of Fiona's previous models were as good. Under Jann's influence, the paintings evolved and changed; Jann had a different look every time he sat, and this inspired Fiona to greater originality and moved her away from the tired, insipid paintings she had spent her 30s and 40s painting. The critics claimed they were insipid, at any rate, and Fiona tended to agree, because she found it hard to distance herself sufficiently from her paintings to be critical about them.

For example, she had always painted landscapes in the studio, only venturing outside for thumbnails and sketches; and painted all her portraits in the studio as well. Jann encouraged her to paint portraits outside, and this sparked off a whole new area of creativity for her. She once found Jann digging in the garden, scraping the frost off the soil, and shouted from the French windows, 'Jann, what are you doing out there in shorts, it's February for God's sake.' Jann turned and smiled a broad, perfect-toothed smile and told her it was the best time of year for shorts. 'Cold weather tones the muscles,' he said.

This was a pose that Fiona had recreated in *Garden II*. It became a snow-covered landscape with a frozen pond, a model heron with a stalactite of ice from its beak to the ground, and Jann in front of it all with his trowel.

She was working on *Garden VII* at the moment. 'I like the way you've left lots of brush hairs in the paint,' Jann said, looking over Fiona's shoulder. His habit of doing this infuriated her. 'It echoes my real hair,' he approved.

Fiona opened her mouth to tell him to bugger off and let her get on with it, then realised what he had said and looked more closely at the painting. 'It isn't intentional,' she said, but he was right, the brush seemed to be moulting and there was lots of hair sprouting from the canvas, making the painting earthy and gritty.

'It should be intentional,' Jann said, 'it adds to the reality of it. Makes it alive.' Fiona silently appreciated Jann's critical comments, however much his energy and loudness irritated her. He could never sit still for five minutes, which is not the first characteristic you look for in a model.

Jann took a large blunt knife from Fiona's work table. He tugged the knife across his hair and after several swipes like an executioner chopping a head from its trunk with a blunt axe, handed a ragged sheaf of hair to Fiona. 'Here you are,' he said victoriously, 'mix that into the paint.'

Fiona held the hair in her hand and watched Jann go back to his stool. His hair was so long and shaggy that you could not notice any real alteration in it. She held the warm hair in her hand, feeling it slip under her fingers like silk, then shrugged and started working it into the painting. She had not been doing this for more than a minute when he started talking; she felt herself tense up.

'It could have all kinds of meanings for the painting, you know,' he said in his whining, drawling accent. 'So far you've just painted a representation of me. This could actually *be* me.'

'Shut up and let me paint.' She mixed some more hair into the painting; it took to it surprisingly well, moulding itself into the brushstroke. Inside Fiona's head she heard voices of programmes on artists waffling on about the way you can identify a da Vinci or a Titian from the brushstrokes. She wondered if people would discuss her in the same way in a hundred or a thousand years' time.

II

Some weeks later Fiona was working a full-length portrait of Jann using no paint at all. It was composed entirely of cut pieces of Jann's hair, moulded into shapes and then applied to the canvas using glue. The critics loved it, claiming it was a mixed-media work that mixed media for a purpose, rather than just the sake of it. Fiona completed many more paintings in the same style, with Jann's enthusiastic encouragement; he now had a much shorter hairstyle, and he talked about the works to any journalist or radio interviewer who would listen. As a consequence Fiona received invitations from several galleries in England, Germany and Denmark. Having been largely written off in her 30s, she was gratified to see such a resurgence of interest.

She recognised that this was due to Jann's ebullient, outgoing nature, where he ran after reporters and gave interviews and was plastered all over magazines. Fiona had no interest in doing such things, nor would she have been capable of it, or patient enough, or photogenic enough. Jann loved it and chased after it like a dog after a stick. The magazines and TV channels loved him in return because he was so beautiful. Programme makers salivated over the idea of featuring the energetic, slim, sexy, perfect-toothed Jann and then alternating segments of the interview with loving, close-up shots of the paintings which revealed him in all his hairy, beautiful nudity.

For several months Fiona somehow became the artist of the moment; she knew this would never have happened in her media-unfriendly corduroy trousers and permanent growl. The way she was portrayed was as an enigmatic reclusive figure (she wasn't reclusive or enigmatic, she just didn't like talking to people) and Jann was the face and the voice.

Several new books and TV documentaries were commissioned; forgotten monographs were reprinted; and most importantly, there were more offers to exhibit and more requests from auction houses than she had paintings to go round. All this after twenty years in the wilderness, leaving paintings stacked against the wall because no one was interested in Fiona Clegg any more, the artist who had been a meteoric success in her twenties but who had long had her day.

Fiona licked the end of the brush thoughtfully and looked at Jann. She twisted and shaped the hair to resemble sinews and muscles; she was in the final stages now, and after slowly sticking each piece of hair to the canvas, sat back and looked at the work carefully. It made Jann resemble a bolting horse, half-man half-beast; and although Jann and everyone else who saw it thought it grotesque, it was so striking and powerful that it was made the centrepiece at the Mall Gallery Christmas exhibition.

After a few more minutes he yawned. 'Have you always been a painter?' he asked.

'I was a sculptor to begin with,' she said slowly, loosely gluing the features into his face, just giving enough detail to see what she was doing but not spending too much time over it in case she changed the position slightly and had to do everything again. 'But the sculpturing wasn't getting anywhere and that's when I moved back to painting. I hadn't painted since art school.'

'Where did you study?'

'The Slade. One of the few colleges that still approved of painting.'

'Is that in England?'

'Yes.'

'So why did you want to become a sculptor?'

'Because I wanted to be a butcher.'

'Okay. Is there a connection?'

'Yes. My father was a butcher. When I was little I wanted to be a butcher too, but he told me girls couldn't do that.' Jann laughed.

'I used to hang around in the doorway watching him work; observing him slice the skin from the meat. It's an art, you know, it's as precise and as beautiful as watching a sculptor with a knife. In some ways it's more beautiful.'

'Why?'

Fiona concentrated on the knees and the elbows. Get that right and the rest will follow; put them in the wrong place and the whole figure will collapse. 'A butcher has an array of knives,' she said, 'and he selects the right one as precisely as a golfer chooses clubs. It's sexual, you know, the way a butcher holds the flank of a cow or a sheep and slices across the skin with a cleaver and it falls away in one clean movement. I used to pick the skins up and carry them, like a blanket, across to the waste table.'

'I know what you mean,' said Jann. 'It's like when you have duck in a restaurant and you use a steak knife to slice the skin across and peel it back.'

She nodded. 'Yes, it's just like that.'

'What did he do then?'

'He would put the skinned animal on the slab and the blood

would run away to the drainage channel.'

III

Having given up on popular success, or popular success having given up on her, Fiona spent most of the last twenty years working on her garden. She had made enough money in the years she had been successful not to have to worry about income; when interest dried up and the paintings stopped selling, she accepted the fact and concentrated on achieving her idyllic garden retreat. Visitors to the house could scarcely believe it was the middle of London when they sat outside with a glass of tea and looked around at the plants and bushes, which were carefully designed to appear to be random and naturally sprouting, but which were in fact controlled so as not to overwhelm the layout.

Fiona's early sculptures were dotted about the garden and added to the sense of space and mathematical beauty; the garden was a perfect mix of nature and human intervention. Fiona saw it as her greatest work, because it had taken twenty years to create as opposed to the average three months for a painting; and it was never finished, it required constant attention. Fiona wished she could live for a couple of hundred more years so that she could keep honing it, improving it, and control it over the ebb and flow of the seasons. Her favourite times were the rare winters when there was a thick layer of snow, as it gave a ghostly, magical sheen to the glass ornaments and the decking walkways. The stream of water from the mirror fountain would freeze up and stay cast like a sculpture of a particular moment. Now, in late summer, the garden was less spectacular but she could spend more time in it.

Fiona sat in the wooden swing-seat and looked at the different shapes, colours and textures. She watched the aeroplane trails in the sky as they slowly broke up and disappeared. Tired, she closed her eyes and swung slowly back and forth and listened to the insects buzzing, the lawnmowers whirring in other, distant gardens, the low, constant drone of nature that you hear in gardens in the summer. She smelt the warmth on her face.

IV

Jann jumped up and flexed his legs. 'This is too tiring a position to maintain,' he said, 'it is bad for the circulation.' Fiona sighed and put the pen down. Jann walked across to Fiona with long, loping strides, to stretch the muscles, and looked critically at the drawing. 'This is too anaemic,' he said, looking at the vague pen strokes and the lazy, nebulous wash that Fiona had painted round the figure. 'What ink are you using?'

She did not answer. He picked the brown ink up and put it back down again, then examined the pen. 'Here,' he said, picking up a craft knife, 'use some of this.' He stabbed the knife into his thumb and let blood into the ink pot for a minute or so.

'It doesn't match the ink,' Fiona complained.

'It will when it dries,' Jann said, running back to the stool.

She did not have much peace before he opened his mouth again. 'Why have you stayed in England?' he asked. 'Why have you never lived anywhere else?'

She shrugged. 'I like the air, and the light.'

'We have good air and light in Denmark. And snow.'

She nodded.

'Does the light make a difference to your paintings?'

'What kind of question is that? Everything makes a difference. If I painted this three feet away it would be totally different from how it is here. Or on the other hand, it makes no difference at all; the work is in my head, not in the place where you live or in what you look at. The painting could be of a different person, but it would still be exactly the same.' She drew breath, and felt thirsty. It was unusual for her to speak for such a long time.

'I see,' he said. 'You are the paintings, and the paintings are you.'

She frowned. 'Not really. People would think I was up my own arse if I said things like that.'

'No, this makes the most perfect sense to me. You are expressing yourself in your art, otherwise it would not be any good. What is the point in doing it unless you put yourself into it?'

'Yes,' she said. She felt an unusual warmth towards him, just for a moment. 'You're a good model,' she said. 'I'm feeling very inspired for the evening – '

'Ah, no, unfortunately,' Jann said, 'I have to be out this evening.'

'With a girl.'

'Yes, that is right.'

'Well if you're in by midnight, come down to the studio and we'll start then.'

'Okay.'

Jann did not get in until two, but Fiona was still up, sipping a whisky in the studio. Jann put his head round the door. Against the white wall and the white door his head appeared disembodied; a floating, comical picture of a red drunken face with blonde hair, bobbing up and down against the door like the head of a puppet.

'I am sorry,' said Jann. 'I am late.'

'Never mind,' said Fiona. 'We'll do a couple of hours now.'

Jann nodded and walked cautiously into the room. With the white floor and the white walls he found it difficult to put his feet down without falling over; he could not tell what was floor and what was empty space.

Fiona stared at the canvas. She stared at Jann. Jann had already lost the pose Fiona had sat him in and was lolling his tongue in his mouth, tapping his fingers absently on his knee.

'Sit the way you were sitting,' Fiona snapped.

'Sorry, I thought as you hadn't done anything for half an hour – '

'That's why I need you to sit how you were sitting, so I can get on with it.'

Fiona irritably drew some lines up and down the canvas as Jann wearily, petulantly sank back into the pose. Fiona marched over and straightened him up, making him sit more angularly, placing his knees precisely together, his hands on his knees and his back straight. 'Put more energy into it!' she shouted. Jann sat in such a way that he showed how annoyed he was. 'You're just sitting there,' Fiona said, marching back and disappearing behind the canvas, 'you're not *doing* anything!'

She carried on for a while, then gave up and ran up the steps. When she came back with a drink a few moments later, he was sitting in the pose, correctly this time. 'I'll be good,' he promised, his hands on his knees sincerely, as if praying, his back rigid and earnest.

She twisted her lip at him, downed the drink and tried to work again. She calmed down when the drink surrounded her brain sufficiently to enable her to get on with it, and, when she was in a good mood, she allowed him to get up and stretch and move around every twenty minutes. It'll be all right, she told herself, once she was happy with the diamond shape of the figure in the centre of the canvas and had started to use paint. As usual, she completely diverted from the forty sketches she had completed of him in the same pose; but as usual, needed to have done those forty sketches to reach this point. By the time they finished at three am, she was satisfied.

The next morning she spent several hours trying to get him out of bed, leaving cups of coffee by his bed, each of which went cold, and alternating coffee-making with violent knocking on his door, to which he responded with vacant groans.

'Come on,' she said impatiently 'I need to get on with it.'

Eventually she hauled him downstairs; it was still only about nine o'clock. At lunchtime he went on strike, refusing to do any more, retiring to his room and slamming the door. Fiona was in a fury for the rest of the afternoon, ferociously weeding the lake and removing dead leaves and flowers from the garden. They did another session in the evening and Fiona felt better.

'People keep asking me,' said Jann, 'whether I don't feel funny taking my clothes off in front of a complete stranger.'

'Really,' Fiona murmured. As soon as she heard the noise of his dry lips opening, her stomach clenched. There had been two blissful minutes of silence and she had been able to concentrate. She hovered with the brush over the canvas, waiting for him to get through this latest commentary.

'Yes,' he said thoughtfully, 'but it seems very natural to me. I want to be a work of art, you know, I want to immortalise myself. I mean, I won't be young and beautiful forever. Will I?' he added, when she did not respond.

'No.'

'So if I want to be a work of art, it means I have to pour my whole being into it, all of it, my body, everything.'

'Right,' Fiona said, trying to make her voice turn down at the end to finish the conversation. She painted some simple areas of broad wash of flesh while he was talking; she tended to do this wherever possible when he talked, then did the more intricate work when he shut up.

'After I'm dead I want people to look at a painting of me and say, "that's Jann Thorsen. He was a famous model". Like the Mona Lisa. The Mona Lisa is the work of art, not the person, but she was a person once. No one thinks of her as a human being, she *is* the art, she's perfect. I'd like that.'

Fiona grunted in response. He never takes the hint, she

thought.

'This is why it's important that I'm with a recognised, famous artist; there's more chance of your stuff being in galleries and being preserved. And the more of me you do, the more chance there'll be of you doing a really successful one of me.'

Fiona put her brush down. 'Not if you don't keep the fuck quiet there won't be.'

V

'You don't do it all yourself, do you?' asked Jann, looking down the length of the garden.

'Yes, of course I do. You haven't seen anyone else coming in, have you?'

'No, I guess not. It must take you ages to look after it.'

'My mother was a gardener. She taught me everything I know. The secret's in the compost. Get the compost right and you won't have any trouble. The garden kept me distracted when there weren't any commissions coming in. You can easily devote the whole day to it you know. Often now when I'm in the garden I speed up because I think, I've got to get on with some painting; and equally, when I'm painting, I don't think I'm doing enough gardening.'

Jann nodded, yawned and leant against the doorframe. 'What's that blue stuff at the front?' he asked lazily.

'Hyssop. Those pink flowers are evening primrose.'

'And that stuff over there?'

'Hydrangea.'

He nodded. He found it hard to connect the names with the flowers. They were just words; and the flowers were just flowers. Why was it that when you see something, you want to know what it is called? Why does everything have to be identified and labelled; why can't you just see blue flowers and pink flowers and be content with that?

Towards the end of the garden Fiona had runner beans climbing up bamboo canes and rhubarb, sprawling in a corner. 'It's a very *English* garden,' commented Jann.

'Yes,' said Fiona, putting her hands in her cardigan pockets, 'I suppose so. I've just done what I know.'

'I guess.'

They walked past the pond which was covered in reeds and had dead twigs floating on the top. 'That's this afternoon's job,' said Fiona as she looked critically at it.

At the end of the garden, the compost heap bulged untidily over its rough wooden frame. 'All the garden waste goes in here,' Fiona told him. 'Everything from the kitchen too. Anything organic.'

He nodded. She watched him carefully. 'You leave it a few months and then spread it on the soil.'

Jann wrinkled his nose up. 'It must be very smelly.'

Fiona picked up a handful of compost and ran it through her fingers. 'No,' she said, lifting it up to her face. 'It smells of rich, beautiful earth.' She held it out to Jann, who sniffed it cautiously and then raised his eyebrows in surprise. 'Yes, you're right.' Fiona squeezed the compost into finger-shaped sausages in her palm, then dropped it back in the rough wooden frame and wiped her hands on her trousers. Her fingers had a perfect crescent of black under the nails, as if they had been painted. 'You've got strong hands,' Jann said, admiring them.

'Have you ever tried sculpting stone with a chisel?' she demanded. Jann shook his head. 'It gives you strong hands.'

Jann reached down and touched one of the large rhubarb leaves. It felt rough and leathery and the veins were like bones. It did not feel anything like he expected it to; he had never touched rhubarb before.

'People waste money on shop fertiliser,' Fiona said. She looked down at the rhubarb and her cracked yellow teeth glistened in a rare smile. Jann looked at her old cardigan and worn corduroy trousers, covered in compost. The strong hands reached down and touched the leaves tenderly.

'I wish I'd had a mum like you,' Jann said. 'We lived in a flat. We didn't have a garden. We had a tray of plants.'

'Your parents are both dead aren't they?'

Jann nodded. 'That's why I'm glad I'm living here.'

She shrugged. 'You could afford your own house now, if you wanted one.'

'Yes, I know.'

Fiona straightened up and turned towards the house. Jann followed her. 'Do you have any children?' he asked. Fiona shook her head. 'Were you ever married?' This is a big house for a single person.'

'That's because I was successful,' replied Fiona.

They walked back into the flat through the plate glass door. 'Did you design this house yourself?' Jann asked, following her down the shallow pine steps into the kitchen. Fiona nodded. She put the kettle on its stand and took a mug from the cabinet.

'Why don't you drink tea, I thought all English people drink tea,' said Jann as Fiona put some coffee in the mug.

She nodded. They watched the kettle boil.

VI

Jann watched Fiona as she expertly racked up a canvas. 'I thought it would take you a lot longer than that,' he said.

'It used to,' she acknowledged, a knife between her teeth. She slit the last two sides of the canvas, stretched the corner over the frame and hammered tacks into the back. The skin of the canvas hung roughly over the back of the frame, like a dead animal hide on a rack.

'I only started making them myself because they were so

expensive to buy,' she said. 'I used to paint over two thirds of my paintings, before I earned any money. She flipped the canvas over and laid it face-down, then hammered the rest of the tacks in more fully when she was sure it was stretched properly.

'Is it better quality if you make it yourself?' Jann asked between the hammering.

'This isn't the best. I refuse to spend good money on it.' The veins stood out on Fiona's forehead.

As often happened, the triangular pose of Jann with his hands on his knees led to a spin-off idea which Fiona wanted to preserve whilst it was fresh and interesting. It was a similar pose, but Fiona was now using a large proportion of Jann's body fluids in the painting, which she kept in jam jars on the workbench; sweat, urine and blood, which she scrupulously collected from him each day. Fiona, sitting irritably behind the canvas, listened to Jann droning on and on about how significant a development in Western art this was, and tried to stop herself getting wound up. She realised how much she needed Jann; none of this inspiration would have occurred to her had it not been for him, and she could not imagine many models being willing to piss in a jam jar for her. She just wished he could be less annoying. She told herself the results were always worth it, and wondered if it was worth trying to paint with music in the background; maybe that would distract him and shut him up.

Her work was flowing now, she realised as she stirred some pubic hair into the paint. She couldn't risk Jann throwing a fit and walking out. She examined the paint carefully before she applied it. It looked superb on the canvas; it gave it life and vitality.

That painting eventually became *Angel in shit* and was auctioned at Bonham's for over a hundred thousand pounds. At the private view, Jann took great delight in pointing out to various fascinated critics where his blood and sweat were incorporated into the painting. He flitted about between paintings like a butterfly trying to choose the brightest flower to settle on.

From a safe distance, Fiona watched Jann chatter, waving his wine glass around in front of *Body: IV*. A pack of critics clustered round him like a litter of puppies. In the painting Jann was leaning on a window-sill looking out wistfully at the rich, green profusion of Fiona's garden. His skin was bluish-white, almost translucent, and he was standing on tiptoes, the tendons in his neck and feet stretched as he gazed longingly towards the end of the garden. It was one of the few works on display that had been made using just paint. In its white frame, against the stark white of the gallery which was so white it was almost green, it looked like a window with a jungle outside, tendrils desperate to burst into the gallery and choke its occupants.

Fiona caught the tail-end of Jann's excited conversation, as she went to find another drink. From the corner of her eye she saw a cool young critic with thick black glasses and a stupid goatee beard making a beeline for her, so she diverted closer to Jann than she would have liked in order to avoid him.

'...he *is* the garden, he *is* nature. The nature outside is unstoppable, much more interesting than his boring life inside the house, and he wants to be part of that nature...' Jann's eyes shone and sparkled.

The critics all scribbled furiously in their notebooks. Fiona left them to it and got drunk.

VII

At two am Fiona drained her whisky and tried to persuade herself that she was tired. She got up and looked at the current canvas of Jann; his eyes stared insolently from it. She looked at it angrily and Jann seemed to sneer contemptuously back at her. Picking up a knife from the table, she slashed the painting vertically and looked at it somewhat unsteadily. She put her hand against it and her fingers moved through the wound; the canvas flapped around her fingers. Jann's body caved in around her hand; it was dead now, not insolent, and there was no mouth to jabber endlessly at her any more.

His door was ajar as always. She walked in and looked at him lying naked under the sheet, his hair lying spread across his back, the blue light of the moon illuminating him.

Fiona had an urge to start painting him. She sat on the edge of the bed and looked at him uncertainly. Just lying there, doing nothing, he was presenting a work to her; she knew exactly how to make what she was seeing into a piece of art. It would take no effort on her part at all; he was a gift. She was frustrated by this. Jann was the artist, not her. He was doing the work, he was the painting; she was just the catalyst, the mechanic, that enabled it to happen. If Jann disappeared, her talent would disappear with it. What the critics didn't realise, Fiona felt, was that she had lost her ability many years ago and now she was just acting as the medium through which Jann's genius was presented to the public. Jann was in control.

As she looked at him, he stirred in his sleep and woke up, and turned to look at her. 'Hello,' he said, in his soft, gravelly, coffee-stained voice.

Fiona opened her mouth to speak but could think of nothing to say. She needed Jann to speak for her.

'Well,' Jann said, sitting up in bed and rubbing his eyes. 'Just as I thought you weren't going to try after all.'

The sheet fell away from him and she looked at his naked torso, gleaming in the blue light. 'You take your time, don't you?'

he murmured.

'I…' Fiona said. 'I just…'

'It's all right,' Jann said, his teeth shining a brilliant white, 'it's okay, I understand. Come on, it's fine.'

Jann's words calmed Fiona down. She felt less oppressed, less wound up, by his soothing words. She reached her hands out, gently stroked his neck, and strangled him.

VIII

Fiona's summer exhibition was a success. Everyone wanted paintings featuring Jann, and to know what Fiona was working on at the moment. But in an exclusive interview with *Wallpaper*, she said that she was ceasing painting and that the current series of works would be her last. They were her best works, she said, and she could go no further. Inevitably, this made the price of the current set of works rocket astronomically. There were requests from Tate Modern, the Pompidou and the Rijksmuseum. Fiona retired to spend her days working on the garden.

Fiona had six new canvases of a uniquely fine quality stacked up in her cellar. She was pleased with them; they were better than anything you could buy. She decided that one day, when she wasn't busy in the garden, she would return to them and paint something, perhaps in memory of Jann. She was not sure yet what she would do, but knew she had to make sure the canvases became something special. Fiona touched them, feeling their silky smoothness under her hands, and the skin sprang back underneath her touch.

The house rang blissfully with silence. She opened the plate window, looked down the garden and saw that it was blooming, alive, enriched. She walked to the end of the garden and ran a fork through the fresh compost, which squelched under the stabbing metal. Slowly she started spreading the rich soil into the earth.

After half an hour she stood up, digging her hands into her lumbar region and grimacing as she felt the bones crack and creak down her spine and across her back. She reached her arms out and stretched her hands as far as they would go. She saw the bones in her fingers, visible because the skin was red and translucent, lit up by the fierce sun like in an x-ray. The fingers reminded her of the strong butcher's hands of her father.

young love

I

The girl in the chip shop smelt of grease and chicken fat. She had heavily made-up eyes, with long lashes, and her eyelids were like hoods, and Jon was in lust with her.

When she looked at him, he was like a mouse before a snake. His heart beat furiously and he did not know what to say.

'What do you want?' she said impatiently. Her words dripped into his ears like honey.

He swallowed involuntarily a couple of times, then managed to say, 'Chips.'

'Just chips?'

He nodded.

She opened a glass flap on the counter in front of her, and picked up a huge gleaming silver spatula. She shovelled enthusiastically into the mountain of chips, tipping them on and off until she harvested a shovelful that marginally overflowed the spatula. Jon stood watching her. Her face shone with grease. The white strip lights showed up the creases in her face where thin rivulets of sweat lay.

Her starched blouse was stretched across her breasts. Each time she moved forwards and backwards a small hole materialised and dematerialised between the second and third button of the blouse. Through the hole Jon could see a bulge of white lace. He stared, mesmerised.

There was a buzzing, crackling sound above him. He looked up and saw a blackened fly drop through the metal grille of the blue neon lamp.

'Here's your chips,' the girl said. Her words reverberated through his brain. She vigorously shook large quantities of salt and vinegar into the bag without asking if he wanted them. A small muscle bulged from the short sleeve of her blouse as she expertly manipulated the vinegar. The chips soaked up the liquid and curled fatly round one another.

She spun the paper bag until it sealed itself. The bag had two little white ears like the edges of a knotted handkerchief.

'That's 40p,' she said. Jon fumbled in his pocket and gave her two shiny 20p coins. The coins were brand new; they'd only come out that year. They were strange little things. Like coins from a foreign country. With eight sides... seven? Six? You couldn't tell without actually counting them, and then you'd forget where you started and lose count.

She blinked and turned to the next customer. 'What do you want?'

Her breasts strained against the blouse. Jon walked outside and sat on the step, out of the way of the door. A car drove past with loud music thumping against the windows. The music sat in his stomach and bumped along with the car until it had gone. Otherwise the street was quiet. A rush of breeze passed through the trees from time to time.

Vinegar-sodden chips lay snugly with each other like old, fat, pale bodies. Jon picked the first one up and one of his eyes involuntarily closed as the vinegar fumes entered it. He could hear the chimes of the church clock striking four, carried to him faintly on the wind. He ate the chips slowly and as the grease lined his lips he thought of the girl in the shop.

Ten minutes later he was still there and the crisp, dark chips at the bottom of the bag were cold. He picked one up by licking his finger and sticking it well down into the bag. The tips of his fingers stung as the salt on the chips got under the nails.

The door rattled and he heard footsteps on the stone steps. 'You still here?'

He dropped the chip he was holding and pushed himself round to look up at her. She stood with her hands on her hips, her hair falling down over her face, and a shapeless black bag about to drop from her shoulder. Behind her the chip shop man stared at Jon through the door as he bolted the locks. His face blurred behind the glass.

'I'm waiting for my Dad,' Jon said. 'He's picking me up. He was meant to be here at four.'

'Oh.' She spoke quietly. The voice didn't make his heart jump so much now. He stood up and wiped his greasy hands on his knees the way his Dad did after he'd been working on the car. 'Might as well walk,' he said, looking thoughtfully into the distance as if contemplating an Arctic expedition.

'Where do you live?' She stepped down onto the road.

'Weller Road.'

'Weller Road?' Her voiced lifted up like a siren. 'You can't walk there. I'll give you a lift if you like.'

His heart beat furiously. He tried to make his reply sound nonchalant. Nonchalant was his word of the moment. 'All right,' he said.

She walked down the road and Jon followed her. Her heels clicked on the tarmac. Her tight white skirt rode up her legs and he could see the outline of her knickers underneath it. There was a large smudge of tomato ketchup on the bottom of the skirt, tight against her thigh. The smudge carried past the skirt and onto her tights.

Her car was an old blue Fiesta. Jon stood beside it, staring at it. 'Doors aren't locked,' she said. Inside it smelt of stale smoke.

When he pulled the door shut the handle fell off in his hand. He felt himself turning crimson.

She burst out laughing, a deep, nicotine-stained, grown-up laugh. 'It does that,' she said. She reached across him, took the handle from his open palm and pushed it back on its square metal rod. Jon stayed motionless in his seat, frozen. He felt his skin tingle as she stretched across him, her right hand pressing down on his knee as her left hand fixed the handle.

She sat back in her seat, rifled about in the door compartment and found a pair of sunglasses. 'Off we go,' she said as she put them on. When the car started the radio came on straightaway. It was halfway through that song by Soft Cell and was at top volume. The bass thumped through the car as it spun into the road like a funfair ride lifting from the ground.

She drove in the centre of the road, only coming back into the left lane if another car approached. 'These roads are so bad,' she explained, 'there's so many holes by the kerbs. Bugger the wheels up, see.'

Jon nodded. She was right; she drove so fast that any holes in the road sent a jarring shudder throughout the car. The trees went past in a summer evening blur. Jon bounced up and down on his seat. She drove with her left hand on the gear stick, her right hand just touching the bottom of the steering wheel.

II

Jon directed her to his house and the car bounced as it hit the kerb at the bottom of the drive.

'There you are,' she said.

'Thanks.' He got out, opening the door with care.

She reversed out of the drive, the car whining as it was pushed back too fast, and then sped off. Jon heard the sound of the car echoing across the road and bouncing off the walls of the house opposite. He stood for a few moments breathing deeply, then an enormous wave of depression overwhelmed him as he turned round and looked at his house. The bland, white-washed walls looked back at him; he studied the paint peeling on the windowsills where the wood was going rotten. The drab, blue paint was flaking away so badly that one could see the brown paint that he remembered from when he was little.

This was also flaking badly; one could see the wood under it. Jon was trying to use 'one' instead of 'you' as someone had told him it was sophisticated. He went round to the back door. The front door was never used as it was theoretically for visitors, although in practice no visitors would be able to get in as it had four bikes piled up behind it. He pushed at the back door and after a few shoves it opened. To begin with the top opened freely, but the bottom stayed wedged. The trick was two or three sharp shoves with the lower arm whilst kicking it at the base.

He heard Dad's voice emanating from within. 'Don't force it!'

Dad was sitting in the kitchen, holding two broken pieces of shower head and trying to fit them together. A screwdriver and two screws rolled around on the kitchen table. Dad looked up at Jon as he walked in.

'This shower head's broken,' Dad said.

'I thought you were coming to get me,' Jon said as he put the TV on.

'Oh yes. Yes, I was just doing this, then I was going to leave. Straightaway.'

III

The next day after school, Jon didn't go straight home. Toby was surprised; they usually walked up to the sweet shop together, then went their separate ways as the roads forked. Toby lived down in Kennedy Road.

'Why?' he asked.

'Why what?'

'Why aren't you coming?' he said patiently. Toby was always very patient; this was one of the reasons Jon liked him.

Jon put his hands in his pockets. 'I feel hungry, see. Going to get some chips.'

'All right. See you.'

'See you.'

He walked off, lifting his bulky bag onto his shoulder every few yards as the strap slipped down his arm.

Jon walked down to the town centre. He wasn't actually hungry; in fact the very thought of chips made him feel ill. He stood outside the demolished building for a few moments and looked inside. There were weeds growing out of the floor tiles. Jon thought this was quite curious. He tried to imagine flowers growing out of the carpets at home.

The building was silent, cavernous; the hot sun shining down on the furniture made it look pale and colour-faded. The wall was orange. This also surprised Jon. There was something naked, unexpected about being able to see into the room, to see the furniture, to see the orange wall. The people who had lived there would have thought they would be the only people ever to see their orange wall and brown furniture; or at least, the only people apart from those whom they invited into their home. Now it had people walking past every day, peering in, looking at everything that was private and coming to their own idle conclusions about the people who lived there. Jon could stand and look in for as long as he liked and no one told him to go away. He found this an irresistible sensation.

He leant against the wire netting that had been slung up to keep people out. The wire pressed into his face. The air smelt sweet, of nettles and discarded orange peel. In the distance, Jon heard an ambulance siren faintly wailing. He tried to climb up onto the netting but it sagged with his weight and the holes in the netting were too small to get his toes into. He jumped away and walked along the path, trying to kick the clumps of grass in the cracks in the pavement so they would detach in one go.

The smell of the fat from the chip shop reached him before he had even turned the corner of the road. As he walked towards it he could see the girl behind the counter. The windows of the shop were dirty and her face kept smudging and then clarifying as he got nearer.

Inside, she was serving someone else, but the man was free. Jon pretended to be looking at the menu. This was not very convincing because the board was just covered in old, rubbed-out chalk. As soon as the girl had served the other customer and slowly counted his money into the till, Jon stood in front of her.

'Oh, right,' she said, when she registered it was him. She sniffed and wiped her nose on her hand. 'What do you want?'

'Chips.'

'Oh yeah. The chips boy.' She opened the glass flap and reached into the chips with the spatula. Her body jerked back and forth as she scooped the chips. There was an intent and alluring frown on her face.

'Do you always just have chips?' she asked, putting her head on one side like an inquisitive dog.

'I can only really afford just chips.' He was conscious of the fact that this was the longest sentence he had ever spoken to her. He flushed.

'Oh,' she said. She was wearing a different blouse today. It wasn't as tight as yesterday's and didn't open up in the middle when she leant forward. Her breasts were more bulbous against the more giving fabric.

'I finish at four,' she said conversationally as she rhythmically shook the salt cellar over the chips.

'Do you?' Jon said, resting his fingers loquaciously on the counter. Loquaciously was his other word of the moment.

'Yes,' she replied, slamming the salt on the formica and picking up the vinegar, 'I always do, during the week. This other girl does the evenings.' She tipped the vinegar into the chips, shaking it up and down expertly to try to make it come out more quickly.

She spun the bag round and handed it to him. 'Here's your chips,' she said.

'Thanks.' Jon handed her four ten pence pieces. She counted them slowly into the cash register. She turned round. There were no other customers waiting.

'Thanks,' she said. She smiled. Suddenly she wrinkled her nose and gasped, as if she was about to sneeze. She looked up at the light, but no sneeze occurred. She opened her eyes wide, as if looking around to see where it had gone.

Jon tried to think of something to say. 'Thanks,' he said. He went out of the door and looked at his watch. It was a quarter to four. He sat on the step, out of the way of the door, and opened the bag. He smiled. Nestling on top of the chips was a battered sausage.

He was trying to eat the last few chips very slowly when he heard the door rattle behind him. 'Still here?' she said.

He turned round suddenly, as if surprised. 'Oh, right, hello,' he said casually. 'Yes. Still here.' He coolly ran a hand through his hair.

She nodded towards him. 'You've got chip fat in your hair.'

'Oh,' he said.

'Do you want a lift home?'

'Well, I can walk,' he said, 'it's not that far.' He narrowed his eyes as if contemplating which way to tackle the Matterhorn and settling for the north face.

They walked towards her car. He walked alongside her this time; this meant that he couldn't look at her bottom, but on the plus side it meant that he was walking with her. He knew the girl from the chip shop. She drove him home again this afternoon. Oh, the girl in the chip shop. Yes, I know her. She gives me lifts now and then.

He listened to the rhythmic nylon scratching of her legs crossing each other as she walked. 'Thanks for the sausage,' he said.

'That's all right.' She smiled at him.

She was parked in the same place. He opened the passenger door and got in first. There were three crumpled-up cigarette packets in the glove compartment.

'I've got to get something from my mum's first,' she said. 'That's on the way to yours. Then I'm going to my dad's. That's past yours. You're not in a rush, are you?'

'Oh, well,' he said, looking at his watch, 'not particularly.'

She drove up Corner Road and Wickham Street, roads Jon had never been along before. She parked at the end of the terrace. They went in. There was a scattering of letters on the floor. She picked them up and put them on the kitchen table.

Her bedroom was in the loft. There were no windows and one light bulb with no shade in the centre of the low ceiling. There was a huge pile of records on an old coffee table. Jon sat on a beanbag.

She went round the room, picking up discarded underwear and shoving it into open drawers. He watched her.

'Mum's not back yet,' she said, as she picked up jeans and a blouse from the floor and threw them in the corner.

'What's the thing you've got to get?' he asked.

'What? Oh yeah. Er, it's downstairs. I'll pick it up before we go.' She took a record from the pile and looked at it thoughtfully. 'Do you like Blondie?' she asked, turning to him.

'Yes,' he asserted.

She put the record on the turntable and pressed a switch.

'Automatic,' he observed. He was impressed. 'You have to lift mine onto the record. It makes a terrible noise if you've got the volume turned up.'

'Yes,' she said, pulling a canvas chair over and sitting next to him. 'I used to have one like that. It was bollocks. My dad bought me this. He works in London, he only comes back to his house weekends. That house is always empty too. You should come round.'

'Yes,' he said. They listened to *Heart of Glass* and then *Call Me*.

'That's a horrible school uniform,' she said.

'I know. I'm going to leave this year, I'm not going to do A levels.'

She reached out towards him, loosened his tie and pulled it over his neck. She threw it on the floor. 'That's better,' she said.

'Thanks.'

'Would you like a cigarette?'

'Yes,' he said, and wondered what it would be like.

She leant onto the floor, picked up a denim skirt and fished out a crumpled packet. She pushed a cigarette into his mouth and put another one in her own. Both cigarettes were bent in the same place. There was a lighter in the packet as well. She lit her own first, then his.

He breathed slowly and cautiously. It left an aftertaste in his mouth like metal, but it didn't make him cough like it did in *Grange Hill* when someone smoked for the first time.

Jon turned to look at her. The shapes of her nipples were imprinted against her shirt. Jon found this odd. He hadn't been aware that you could make out her nipples in that particular shirt. Perhaps it was the light.

He tore his gaze away from her breasts and looked up at her face. She was studying him with pursed lips. She smiled. She froze for a second, then reached to the bottom of her blouse with both hands and pulled it over her head. She dropped it onto the floor and stared at him, unblinking. She breathed audibly and her heavy breasts moved up and down.

Jon nonchalantly put the cigarette back in his mouth and

inhaled deeply. He coughed and choked and his throat constricted as if it were ingesting hot tarmac.

The girl lifted her chin up. The light from the bulb gave a yellow glow to her naked neck. She was wearing a black bra. Her skin bulged out from each side of the tight straps. 'You can touch if you want to,' she said quietly, half-smiling. Jon loquaciously tipped cigarette ash into a cup.

She leaned towards him, paused for a second, then kissed him slowly on the mouth. He smelled her hair. It smelt of chips. She kissed him a second time and this time he opened his mouth. Her breath smelt sweet, smoky and grown-up.

Her tongue darted into his mouth, flicked around his teeth exploratively and then vanished. Jon felt the hairs on his back prickle as if a cold wind had passed through them. He kissed the side of her mouth. There were a few tiny hairs above her lip which tasted of sweat. There were some slight bumps below her mouth that looked as though they might turn into spots. He kissed them.

She stood up and took hold of his hand. She led him to the bed. They both tipped the records, clothes and shoes onto the floor. Jon lay on the bed and the girl lay on top of him. He could feel her pressing into different parts of his body. He touched her breast. He was surprised to find how soft it was and yet firm at the same time. He tried to think what it was like. Blancmange, he concluded.

'So how old are you?' he asked.

'Nineteen,' she said.

He studied the ceiling. There was a spider's web in the corner of the room. Nineteen, he thought. He was lying on a bed with the girl from the chip shop in her mum's house and she's nineteen, and I'm touching her breast, and it's five o'clock in the afternoon. Wow.

'What's your name?' she asked.

'Jon.'

'Mine's Lisa.'

She pulled her skirt off and unzipped his trousers. Her hand wrapped around his cock like a snake winding round a tree. The hand was cold and still slippery with grease. She reached down to his balls. The nothingness between his cock and his bottom, an area he thought did nothing and had no name and which he had never thought about before, suddenly felt as if it were being pulled up from inside him.

They rolled over and her hair flayed out behind her like she was floating in a swimming pool. Jon leant down and kissed her face beneath the warm hair. He could taste her breath. It made his mouth water. A stray, chip-soaked hair slid into his mouth.

She had a large, black mole on her shoulder. Jon rubbed his nose against it. He reached down between her legs and stroked the hair. It was wet and rough and sprang back against his hand. He lay on top of her and moulded into her dampness. In the dark corner of the unclean room, the web vibrated and a spider slowly descended.

IV

She drove him home. She almost hit a car when she pulled out of her road because she didn't look properly. As she drove he put his hand on her leg.

'Got to work at eight o'clock tomorrow,' she said.

'Do you like working?'

'It's all right. The man's all right. He pays me in cash. I think he's a bit dodgy. Doesn't matter though. I'd rather have cash anyway.'

She hit the kerb and bumped into Jon's drive. It was seven o'clock.

'Thanks,' he said. She winked at him and blew him a kiss. He felt vital internal parts of himself sinking down towards his genitals. He turned towards the house, panic-stricken that someone might see. There was no-one at the windows though.

He watched her drive away. She held the wheel with one hand and dexterously removed a cigarette from its packet with the other. As she turned the corner he heard a squeal of brakes.

Jon forced his way past the back door and entered the kitchen. Dad was staring out of the window. The kettle was going full blast and the lid was rattling as it was about to boil. Dad turned to look at him.

'I've just put the kettle on,' he said.

'Yes,' Jon concurred.

Dad turned back to look down the garden. Jon followed his gaze. The garden was unmown as far as the beanpoles, which leaned at slightly different angles in the soil like gondola poles in Venice. After that, the garden became completely unkempt and was full of rubbish. Old upended wheelbarrows, a pile of compost overgrown with grass, and a burnt-out oil drum that Dad used to burn rubbish in. There was a very narrow pathway cut through the rubbish down to the shed. The green paint on the shed door was cracked and peeling away. Underneath you could see the old yellow paint, which was flaking away too, so that you could see the wood. Jon and his Dad stared at the garden for a few minutes, then Dad got up to make some tea.

'Where have you been all afternoon then?' he asked.

'I went for some chips,' Jon said.

Jon lay upstairs on his bed and his whole body seemed to glow. It tingled in different places all at once. He opened the window and took his shirt off and let the cool breeze from outside flow all over him. He would never forget April 3rd. He knew that he would look back on this day as the most significant one of his life, with the possible exception of December 4th 1977 when he won a Blue Peter badge.

Jon realised that Lisa hadn't taken whatever it was she needed to take to her Dad's. He wished he had remembered when he was still in the car; he could have reminded her. He hoped it wasn't anything important. He lay in bed and whispered the word 'Lisa' over and over again.

V

Because of school, he only saw her about once a week. He had 'O' levels to worry about. During the summer he saw more of her, but she liked going to the pub on work evenings with her friends. Jon didn't think he'd feel comfortable in there with a lemonade.

Mostly he saw her during the days. They often slept together in her loft during the afternoon. The square of sky through the small window was always a slab of unclouded blue. The air in the room was hot and thin and they used to sweat together on her cotton sheets. She washed her sheets every other week and when he buried his face in her pillow he could smell her hair. When he got home he could always smell her on his clothes.

He worried that his Dad would say something. He must have noticed something was different. Often Jon didn't get home from school until seven or eight o'clock. On one occasion he did ask what Jon had been doing. Jon said he'd been in the park.

'That's good. A boy your age should get lots of air. Were you running?'

Lisa and Jon didn't have much to say to each other, but that didn't matter. He used to sit on the beanbag and she'd play records at top volume and dance in front of him and sometimes take her clothes off while she danced. John would never be allowed to play music that loud at home, but Lisa's mum was never there to tell her to turn it down. Occasionally, after an hour or so, there would be a banging on the wall from next door. Only then would Lisa switch the music off and they'd lie in her bed in silence, tightly wrapped up in her sheets, getting hotter and sweatier and running their fingers over each other's bodies.

'Doesn't it bother you that your mum's never here?' he said.

She wrinkled her nose up. 'Not really. I'm not a kid any more. Sometimes she doesn't come back all night.' She yawned. Jon saw her tonsils. 'I prefer the quiet anyway,' she continued. 'I'd probably move out if my mum was here all the time.'

The autumn was still hot. Lisa developed a strange habit of wanting to turn the lights off each time they had sex. Whenever he went round there in the afternoons the blind was down on the skylight.

'I looked in the mirror and felt fat,' she explained. Jon ran his hand over her bottom. 'No you're not,' he said.

'It's just a phase,' she said.

Phases were things girls had; Jon knew he would look more grown-up if he just acknowledged it instead of complaining that he wanted to see her naked. He nodded.

'You don't mind do you?'

'No, of course not,' he said laconically. At least, he thought he meant laconically. Phases ended, after all. They lay together curled up in the darkness of a sticky September afternoon and Jon felt even more excited that he couldn't look at her. She moved like an animal and he had to anticipate her. His sense of touch became more acute as his vision had been lost. They explored things they would never have found just by looking for them.

VI

A week after Christmas he walked into the chip shop. There was a new girl behind the counter. She had red hair and a sour expression. 'Yes?' she said. Jon frowned.

'What happened to the girl who used to work here?'

'Dunno,' the new girl replied.

'Will she be in tomorrow?'

'Dunno.'

The chip shop man came from behind the counter, wiping his hands on his apron. 'Now young man,' he said. 'You'd better be off.' He put a hand on Jon's shoulder. His large, fat fingers were like five uncooked sausages. He leant in towards Jon. His breath smelt of beer.

'Why?' Jon asked. 'What's happened to Lisa?'

'You shouldn't get yourself mixed up with people like that,' he said.

'People like what?'

The man was gently pushing him towards the door. Jon did not resist him. He felt sick that Lisa wasn't there, and he didn't want to stay in the shop any longer.

'Don't you read the papers?' said the man.

'No.'

'Hasn't anyone talked to you?'

'No. Should they have?'

'Good,' he said. He opened the door and held it for Jon, as if Jon were an old woman.

'You run home and don't think about it any more,' he said. 'And don't say anything.'

'What do you mean, don't say anything?' said Jon, looking at the man diffidently. Diffident was his new word. 'Don't think about what?'

'Well,' said the man. 'Don't mention chips, anyway.'

VII

Jon walked to Lisa's mum's house. He felt reassured that Lisa would be there when he saw the car in the drive. He knocked on the door. After a few moments the door opened, but it wasn't her. A woman who looked about thirty-five came to the door. She had uncombed blonde hair and the skin around her eyes was red. She was too young to be Lisa's mother, Jon thought.

'Is Lisa here?' he asked.

The woman looked at him. 'Oh, you're the one are you?'

'What one?' he said. 'Is Lisa here?'

'No,' said the woman. 'She isn't.'

'Oh,' he replied.

She sniffed. 'You better come in.' She turned and walked back down the hallway. Jon peered down the empty darkness of the corridor, then followed her.

The house smelt stale, like the smell when you get back from holiday and no one's opened the windows all week. The woman was sitting on the sofa, smoking a cigarette. She didn't look up at Jon, she just glared at the fireplace and smoked. She smoked the same kind of cigarettes as Lisa.

'Where is she?' he asked.

The woman shrugged. 'I don't know. Nobody knows. The police don't know. The hospital don't know.'

'Hospital?'

Now the woman turned to look at him. 'That's where people tend to leave unwanted babies,' she said.

Jon felt his legs shaking. The air seemed to get thinner. 'I... I... I didn't know that,' he said.

'You must be the last then. It's all over the papers. Funny that. I was second-last.' Jon stared at her. She shrugged in a manner that Jon thought was quite diffident.

'Well,' she said, 'she had the baby and dumped it outside the hospital. She wrapped it up in newspaper. A boy. They expect it'll live. They've called it Brian.' She waited for him to say something. ' "They" being the hospital,' she added from underneath her raw, red eyes.

'What a horrible name,' Jon said.

'What's it got to do with you?'

Jon shifted his weight from one foot to the other. He needed to sit down and he wanted to go to the toilet. He was still shaking.

The woman sniffed. 'So she's run away,' she said, as if summing up.

'But why?' he said. 'Why would she run away?'

The woman's cold eyes glared at him. 'Because if you're fourteen and you have a baby that's what you do.'

The silence burned like snow on the skin. Jon sat down on the chair. He didn't care whether or not he'd been asked to. He raised a hand to his head, but it shook so much he let it drop onto his leg again.

'She can't be,' he said eventually, pleased to have used logic to address the situation.

'What?'

'She can't be,' he said, more loudly.

'Well, she is. Apparently she's been working in a fish-and-chip shop of all things, instead of going to school. I wondered where she was getting the money to buy all those clothes.'

The woman lit another cigarette with jerky, irritated movements and shoved it into her mouth as if it had somehow offended her.

'She told me she was nineteen,' he said.

The woman glared at him. 'Oh for fuck's sake,' she said. 'I wasn't born yesterday. Does she look nineteen?'

Well, yes, actually, thought Jon.

'You needn't bother trying to pull the wool over my eyes,' the woman was continuing, raising an eyebrow at him. 'I'm not stupid.'

She flicked ash at the ashtray. Most of it fell on the coffee table.

'Well,' she continued in a quieter voice. 'Maybe I am stupid. I don't know how she concealed it from me. I suppose I should pay more attention.' She tapped the formica table in front of her. A coffee cup rattled.

'It didn't show,' he said. Jon suddenly remembered the darkened room and the phase. During her phase, she had got a bit bigger; he hadn't wanted to tell her this because he thought she would be upset. And, he realised, he hadn't seen her naked for the last few months.

'Children often do hide it, somehow, when they have them that young. The doctor told me,' she said. Jon's stomach turned.

'And I think she's been stealing from me. Things keep disappearing.' She shook her head and muttered something inaudible.

'At least the car's still outside,' Jon said helpfully, and immediately wished he hadn't.

'What? Oh my God. Don't say she's been driving the car.'

'Er – not really,' he said, truthfully enough.

She was shaking her head again. 'You'd think I'd know my own daughter, wouldn't you? But I didn't. I didn't know her at all.'

She looked as if she was about to cry. Another silence hung in the air, like jelly wobbling.

'Perhaps she'll come back,' Jon said, to comfort her.

'Bloody hell,' the mother said, the cigarette dangling from her mouth in alarm. 'She'd better not.'

Jon stood up. 'Well,' he said. 'I'm going to go now.' He tried to look nonchalent and loquacious.

The woman ignored him. She did not get up. She resumed her contemplation of the fireplace.

VIII

Jon ran all the way home. Half of him was desperate at the thought of what had happened, half of him was desperate that he might never see Lisa again. He couldn't cope with that thought. He didn't care if she was fourteen. He didn't care if she had had a baby. What had it got to do with anyone except him and her?

When he got home Dad was sitting on the stool in the kitchen, gluing a handle onto a teapot. Jon stood in the doorway, breathing heavily. He didn't know what to say.

'This teapot needed mending,' Dad said, looking up at him.

Jon remained in the doorway and flapped his hands. 'Have we got this week's local paper?' he asked eventually.

'Oh, I don't know, son. What day is it today?'

'Thursday.'

'What day does the paper come?' He put the handle against different parts of the teapot to see if it looked right.

The front doorbell rang. Jon froze to the spot. Dad looked up, his eyes swimming about like confused goldfish behind his huge square glasses.

'Who on earth can that be?' said Dad.

Jon went to the front door. He pushed the bicycles to one side and shoved them up against the stairs where they lay like dead animals, their bells ringing faintly and their wheels spinning. He could see two dark shapes looming behind the frosted glass of the door.

When he opened it there were two policemen standing on the doorstep. Jon was not used to the view of the road from the front door. It didn't look right; it didn't look like where he lived. Both policemen were huge, much bigger than normal people should be. Jon looked up at them. 'Hello son,' one of them said.

Jon looked at their crisp white shirts, and at their chins which were covered in black dots from where they had shaved and at the massive guns that hung ominously from their belts. After they had spoken to Dad, who listened in ashen-faced amazement at their story, they showed Jon where to sit in the back seat. He put his seat belt on.

In the house, Dad sat on the stool by the window and stared down the length of the garden. He shook his head from time to time. He went to the phone to ring Jon's mum, but his hand hovered over the dial. He couldn't think what to say to her. He looked at his hand. It was old and lined and covered in marks and creases.

The police car drove slowly into town. It went past the chip shop and Jon tried to see through the murky windows. He watched a fly flash yellow and orange as it was incinerated by the blue neon lamp, then drop blackened and lifeless to the tray below.